Jeb Strauss and the Riches of Water Town

by

John V. Suter

CHAPTER 1

WATER FROM ROCK

The air is thick with a combination of moisture and pollen along the banks of the Etowah River. The kayak drifts along on the slow-moving current as the river nears a sharp bend. Jeb pulls his wide-brimmed hat off his head and squints at the bright sun. He removes his glasses leisurely and wipes the sweat droplets from the lenses. Jeb runs the towel across his face and places his glasses back on the tip of his nose.

The music of the cicadas and the tree frogs fills the air with a rhythmic serenade that rivals the sloshing water against the bank and exposed rocks. This section of the river is remote and serene. He hasn't heard the roar of an automobile in over an hour.

Jeb places his hat firmly on his head and removes a faded map from the bag under his legs. He traces the thin blue line with his finger glancing up at the bank.

"Are we any closer to this supposed honey hole of yours?" Clem growls, swatting at the cloud of mosquitoes hovering over his head.

"Not much farther." Jeb smiles.

"I hope you're right. These filthy bloodsuckers are eating me alive.

"It must be your sugary personality that's drawing them toward you. There aren't any around me."

Clem pants heavily as he waves his arms over his head like the rotor of a helicopter. Jeb chuckles studying his map. Droplets of sweat drip from his nose onto the map, making small circular indentations on the faded paper.

"There it is," Jeb says.

Clem looks ahead. "I don't see anything."

"The untrained eye."

Clem stares at Jeb with his jaw tightly clenched. A fat mosquito lands on his arm, and he jumps backward, nearly throwing himself out of the kayak.

"Easy, killer," Jeb says, grabbing the side of the boat. He points toward the bend in the river. "See that small bar extending into the river."

Clem flails wildly trying to regain his balance. "I don't see anything except these darn mosquitos. I can't believe I let you talk me into coming along with you again."

"We have fun on these little excursions," Jeb replies.

"No."

Jeb laughs. "Of course, we do. As I was saying that little sand bar is where the Amicalola Creek enters the river. If I'm right, then the marker should be where the creek drops through the ridge."

A loud splash interrupts the tranquility of the river, causing Jeb to glance to his left. Water drips from Clem's face, and his paddle floats lazily downstream ahead of his kayak.

"What do you mean through the ridge?"

Jeb folds the worn paper into a square and shoves it into the front pouch of his bag. "Just what I said," Jeb replies, smiling, "You're going to like this ride, but you might want to get your paddle."

Jeb motions toward the paddle, lazily moving farther from their drifting boats. "How did it end up in the river?"

Clem's face reddens, and Jeb sees the veins on the side of his neck pulsating. Jeb is sure that if the paddle had still been in the boat, Clem would try to hit him with it.

"I'm moving ahead. Collect your paddle and meet me up on the Amicalola." He paddles smoothly through the brownish-green water. Small droplets land on his shoulder and legs as he lifts the oar out of the water. He glances back, and Clem's face is redder than ever, and his knuckles are white from gripping the edge of the kayak.

"I'm not getting it for you," Jeb yells, pushing the oar through the cool water. Clem grumbles loudly behind him, but Jeb isn't able to make out the angry words.

Jeb rows along the side of the drifting oar and scoops it from the water. He tosses it over his shoulder without looking. "Don't say I never did anything for you, old buddy," Jeb calls. With a loud splash and a series of distinctive growls, Jeb is sure that his pass was a success. He pushes the oar through the water with more power and speed, wanting to move his kayak at the fastest speed possible.

He needs time to search for the key, and the key is hidden somewhere in the chute of the river as it flows through the ridge. Not knowing the details makes Jeb uneasy. He always likes knowing exactly where the "X" is. That makes hunting for lost things much easier, and it makes succeeding in finding those lost things much more likely. Treasure hunting is always a gamble and a risk. More than likely he will never find anything, but having the best available data increases his odds.

However, this time the research did not produce a definite location. He has found a vague description in the writings of a man named Martyn Hale. He describes a treasure that is hidden in a cave near Walden's Ridge. The treasure was supposedly hidden by Chief John Ross in the 1830s.

Jeb searched every available document, but nothing mentioned a lost treasure until he came across the writings of Martyn Hale. His descriptions and evidence allude to an extensive treasure that the chief hid from the state authorities of Georgia before they could confiscate it. With this tiny sliver of the puzzle in hand, Jeb found that the key to the treasure is hidden in a cave somewhere off the Etowah River.

Jeb paddles forcefully through the plodding current, ducking under branches of privet and rhododendron. The coarse limbs claw at his exposed skin, causing long pink scratches.

Clem grumbles loudly behind him, "You could have put it above the cave."

"Where's the fun in that?" Jeb replies. "Besides, you could use the exercise."

A series of splashes roars from behind Jeb's boat. He turns, and Clem is swinging the paddle high over his head looking deranged.

"These filthy bloodsuckers are driving me crazy!" Clem growls.

"Paddle faster. They won't be able to bite you," Jeb replies, chuckling.

"That's not funny. Get us to the cave or wherever this key is, so we can get out of this wretched place."

Clem swings the paddle wildly around his kayak, striking at the elusive insects. The boat teeters from side to side, causing Clem to drop his paddle.

"Shoot." He gasps, clawing at the water for the lost oar.

Jeb chuckles. "Don't lose that," he says, pushing his oar deep into the drifting current. "It will be hard paddling with your hands."

Jeb smiles as he glides by the creeping branches of oak and poplar trees that shade the creek bank. The temperature is much cooler in the shade, and he steers his kayak toward the bank leaving the sunlit water. A few frogs dart into the cool green water beside him. He looks down and sees them scurrying smoothly through the calm current.

He looks ahead at the sharp bend approaching, and the shadows that extend out into the center part of the creek. The farther up Amicalola Creek they venture, the more shrouded it becomes. Jeb can see the fullness of the forest enveloping the thin waterway, turning the canal into a shadowy pathway through a thick dense wood.

Jeb has paddled this route a hundred times in his mind to prepare for the adventure. Riding the chute through the rocky ridge can be dangerous, so he has gone over the plan. Paddling against the current should allow him to see the opening, whatever size it happens to be.

The chute through the ridge isn't much farther, and he hopes that he doesn't miss the crevice where the key is hidden. He isn't sure how it will look inside, but he envisions carved smooth walls that have been shaped by the flowing water with a small room hollowed out of the rock by the powerful steam.

Shadows creep farther over the waterway, and the canopy above blocks most of the sunlight. Small patches of light shine off the cool water, creating a shimmering light show around his kayak. Jeb pushes the paddle deeper into the water and pulls on the oar with a strong force that propels the boat toward the sharp bend in the stream. His heart quickens, and he licks his lips. In seconds, he presses forward straining against the quickening river current. His boat skirts the inside edge of the bend, and the main current strikes the side of his boat. The kayak rocks from side to side, sending a bit of water into the vessel.

This is going to be more difficult, he thinks as he steadies the boat. The canal through the ridge must have made the current faster. Jeb grits his teeth and powers the kayak farther upstream. His muscles burn, but he sees the frothy water emerging from a sheer column of gray rock ahead.

"We're here!" he yells. He maneuvers the craft toward the dense tree-lined bank out of the swiftly flowing water.

"Clem!" he says without turning around. Splashes come from behind him downstream.

"Every time. Every time," Clem grumbles. He swats at the surface violently sending jets of water high into the air. The water falls onto his head causing more grumbling and more splashing.

Jeb laughs. "Paddle in this direction. The current is a little slower."

"A little slower he says," Clem responds, putting the oar into the water and pulling with all his strength. "This is the last time, Jeb. I promise you this is it."

"You say that every time.

"This time I mean it!"

"Sure, you do." Jeb laughs as Clem struggles with the kayak in the swift current. "Any chance for a gold strike will bring you back again and again."

"Not anymore!"

Clem paddles beside Jeb, breathing heavily wiping the sweat and creek water from his face.

"I will let you rest a minute before we go inside," Jeb says, pointing toward the current flowing out of the rock wall.

The opening in the rock looks like a mine opening, but it isn't rectangular. The water has formed a large oval cut in the rock. Jeb isn't sure how deep the water is, but the top of the rock is maybe five or six feet above the water's surface. He hopes that the chamber is wider inside. It will not be pleasant if the cut through the rock shrinks as they go through.

"You have got to be kidding me." Clem bows his head.

"The key is inside that rock, and we're going in to get it."

"We are going to die."

"Eventually but not today."

Jeb grabs his paddle tightly in his hand and pulls his river hat tightly onto his head. He turns the light on his headlamp on, motioning for Clem to do the same.

"Oh man," Clem says, flipping the switch on his lamp.

"Stay close behind me and keep an eye out for the cavern inside," Jeb says.

"If it exists," Clem replies.

Jeb is confident that Martyn Gale's story is real, and this will be the first leg on a journey that will reveal a treasure that has remained hidden for two hundred years.

Chapter 2

River to Nowhere

The water rushes under the hull of the kayak with swiftness sending a shower of white spray across the top. Jeb pushes his paddle deep in the churning creek, pulling his boat along inch by inch toward the gaping hole in the sheer rock face. The current pulls against him, but he presses forward with strong deep strokes propelling his craft nearer to the looming rocks.

The roar of the water stifles all other sounds along the river. He can't hear his labored breaths escaping from his mouth. Jeb paddles harder and finally enters the mouth of the cavern. The white beam of light from his headlamp dances on the dark surface of the water. The light from the large entrance fades amazingly quickly. The sunlight ventures into the cavern a few feet then disappears entirely.

Jeb paddles ahead into the enveloping darkness. Luckily, the swiftness of the current has subsided, and he looks around at the perfectly smooth walls.

"I would hate to get caught in here," Clem says from behind him. His voice echoes off the stones and reverberates around the boat.

"You don't think the water will rise, do you?" Clem asks.

"No need to worry, Clem," Jeb replies.

"When someone says that, it usually means you should be worrying."

"Not this time."

The tunnel moves in a straight line or what Jeb thinks is straight since it is completely black except for where the beam from his headlamp falls. Jeb scans the walls and ceiling of the cave making sure that his light shines on every surface. Farther and farther, they travel into the cavern through the ridge. Faint sounds of trickling water drift into the tunnel and the distinctive *plops* as the water falls into the creek. Crevices are above them.

"Make sure you look toward the ceiling," Jeb says. He cranes his neck upward, and the small beam of light bounces off the undulating surface of the shiny rock.

The rock formation mirrors the crest and trough of a wave indicating that the water waves have eaten at the solid surface throughout the years.

"I don't see any opening," Clem says somberly. "I bet I'm risking my life for nothing. A stupid story."

"It's here somewhere," Jeb replies, scanning the opposite wall. His headlamp is like a spotlight in the encompassing darkness. He could have missed a crevice or crag somewhere when he was paddling upstream through the dark channel of rock. *It has to be here. Martyn Gale's journal had been specific*, Jeb recites it in his mind. *A hidden stream flows through a vast column of rock emptying into High Town River. Inside the tunnel lies a vast chamber, and this is where I found the key to a Cherokee fortune.*

This has to be the hidden stream, and the key chamber is within this mountain. Jeb paddles slowly, barely overcoming the flow of the water. The round white light from his lamp slowly moves from the side of the cavern up the undulating walls. The cavern is sealed. The solid rock has no gaps or cracks. Jeb grits his teeth moving his head faster across the rock.

The seconds tick by, and they venture deeper and deeper into the tunnel through the mountain. The only sound is Jeb's labored breaths and the paddle slapping against the water. It must be farther inside the ridge. When he read the Hale account, it made it seem like the crevice was near the exit by mentioning the High Town River. As he moves forward, Jeb smiles. If he were hiding a vast treasure, he would make it almost impossible to find. It appears that is what John Ross and his followers had done with this one.

"Jeb," Clem drawls behind him.

"What?" Jeb replies not looking away from the wall.

"We're running out of tunnel!" Clem's voice echoes off the enclosing walls.

"HUSH," Jeb yells.

"We're going to be buried in here. I should have never . . ."

"But you did. Now, be quiet!"

The ceiling presses downward brushing against Jeb's hat. The light from the lamp dances on the wall with each scrape against the rocky roof. Jeb leans backward so the narrow beam of light can drift across the surface of the tunnel. He trains the beam on the tunnel ahead, and the water appears to the rising. As he moves forward, the cavern rumbles. He places his hand against the wall, and a vibration rolls through the smooth rocks. He looks at the water rolling in a rotating pattern like a whirlpool.

Jeb looks around frantically. The opening has to be here somewhere. "What's going on, Jeb?" Clem asks his voice trembling. "I can't get out of this current."

"We're caught in a whirlpool," Jeb replies impatiently.

"Oh jeez… I'm going to drown . . . I'm going to die . . . I can't believe I listened to you."

The kayak spins slowly in a clockwise motion, banging against the rocky wall. Jeb hears the rush of water coming in from somewhere, but the darkness of the cave hides the source from his eyes. He glances at the ceiling, and the rising water pushes him closer and closer to it. The front of the kayak scrapes against the wall causing him to spin uncontrollably.

This is going to end badly if I can't figure a way out of this, he thinks.

The boat slams against the wall violently, screeching loudly with the plastic grinding against rock. Water flows into the boat slowly soaking his shoes and pants. "Just when you thought it couldn't get any worse," Jeb says, smiling.

"I don't want to hear anymore. I want out of here!" Clem screams.

"Look for an opening," Jeb says. "Something is creating this whirlpool."

"If I make it out of here, Strauss. I'm killing you."

"Do something instead of cry."

Jeb lowers his body into the boat. The ceiling is two feet above his head and that distance is shrinking with every passing second. His boat tilts to the right sending more cold mountain water into the compartment. Jeb grabs his pack and places the straps over his shoulders and slips into the swirling water. The coldness bites his at his skin, sending a chill through his body. He kicks his legs forcefully keeping his head above the turbulent water. His kayak slowly sinks beneath the roaring surface.

The water lifts him upward toward the rocky ceiling. The channel fills up fast with the swirling water tossing him in circles like a cork in a whirlpool. He searches along the wall for an opening out.

"You better think of something fast," Clem screeches.

Jeb pulls himself through the water toward the curved wall. He feels a current tugging at his legs trying to drag him under the water. "I'll be right back," Jeb says.

"You'll be . . ."

Jeb takes a deep breath and dives under the rolling white caps. The current rips at his pack and almost plucks the lamp from his hat. He kicks his legs powerfully against the rotating current toward the smooth rock wall. He extends his arms keeping his hands in contact with the wall. He doesn't want to smash face first into the unforgiving stone.

The cold water pulls him backward and deeper. He can't remember how long he has been under the water, but his lungs burn sending jolts of pain across his chest. His heart beats frantically against his ribs like a trapped bird in a cage. An opening has to be somewhere. It is a vertical current that goes somewhere. He hopes that it will take him somewhere other than here.

He searches the wall and the faint light from his lamp passes over a small rectangular opening. He sees the suspended particles flowing into the dark chasm.

"That's it!" Jeb kicks toward the surface, struggling against the downward current. Finally, he breaks the surface, taking in deep gasps of fresh welcome air.

"I thought you were dead," Clem says.

"Not . . . yet . . ." Jeb replies. He takes another giant gulp of air. "I think I found a way out."

"A way out?"

"You'll have to ditch the boat."

"We're going down there," Clem says, pointing under the water.

"It isn't far."

Clem mumbles words that Jeb can't hear and picks up his bag. "I don't really like you right now," Clem says.

"Get in we have to go."

Clem falls out of the boat, sending a spray of water in all directions. He slaps at the water surface like a flailing dog.

Jeb slaps his shoulder. "Follow me." Jeb says with a smile.

Jeb takes in a lung full of air and watches Clem do the same. He dives below the frothy surface and kicks hard against the horizontal current. Jeb looks back, and Clem swims behind him with his cheeks puffed out full of air. They swim toward the rectangular cut in the rock and shoot through the opening, riding the swift current into the darkness.

CHAPTER 3

MESSAGE IN A BOTTLE

They wind their way through the narrow passage, riding the fast-moving current. Jeb's faint light still burns, but he only catches small glimpses of the passing rock. What he sees lets him know that the current is ascending. Within a few seconds, they are thrust into a large cathedral-style opening. The river continues through the high-ceiling cavern, moving at a much slower pace. A small sliver of light filters down into the base of the cave from tiny holes in the rocks of the ceiling. Jeb sees the bright blue sky through the tiny openings. Jeb surveys the wall, and his heart jumps.

"There you are," he says quietly. All along the stone wall, intricate letters are written on the smooth surface of the rocks.

Jeb kicks his legs and propels his body toward the rocky lip of the cavern. He grabs the smooth rocks and hauls himself out of the cool water. The exquisite script delicately drawn on the wall hundreds of years ago brings a smile to his face.

"Can you read it?" Clem chokes behind him.

"This isn't the message about the stash of gold."

"Then why are you so happy?"

Jeb turns and points to the beautiful letters painted on the wall. "This lets me know that Martyn Gale's story is real. His account told of a large amphitheater-like room in the center of a mountain. This room is enormous, yes. The flowing water led to this geologic formation, and inside, there are writings from the Cherokee people. It all fits."

Clem drops onto the stone bench beside the gently rolling river. "While you search for the key or whatever it is, I'm going to close my eyes and try to forget that you almost got me killed." Clem lowers his hat over his eyes and lays out on the cold gray stone.

Jeb turns and stares at the letters studying their shape and slant. The sunlight filtering in from above illuminates the wonderful writing. He pulls open his pack and extracts his field book. He takes the book out of its wet plastic container and hurriedly flips through the pages. He stops abruptly and extracts his pencil from the spine of the book. He places the tip of the pencil in his mouth as he reads through the journal.

Inside the cavern, there is a table-like platform near the center of the room. At the base of the platform, you will find a faded "T" etched in the rock. Behind this stone lies a message from Chief John Ross. His words will lead you to a vast treasure hidden prior to their journey west. I have left the note as I found it so that if I am not successful others can look for the riches.

The sunlight fades inside the cavern, creating a shadow-filled room. Jeb takes the pencil from his mouth and carefully traces the letters from the wall into his journal. His eyes dart from the wall to the dull white paper.

"Hurry up, Strauss," Clem says from the floor of the cave.

"Almost finished," Jeb replies.

"You know how were getting out of here?"

"No idea."

"That's just great," Clem says.

Jeb shoves his journal into his back pocket and steps away from the wall. His footsteps echo off the walls and the ceiling. He walks toward the center of the enclosure where Gale said the stone table would be. Small droplets of water drip on his shoulder from the cracks in the rock overhead. Ahead in the shadows, he sees the smooth flat surface of elevated stone protruding from the smooth floor.

Larger drops of water fall onto the stone table repeatedly. Jeb rubs his fingers together, nervously looking at the small divots the water created in the hard rock. He feels the excitement building inside himself the closer he gets to the prize. This is only the first step along the path to an elusive treasure. Many say that the John Ross treasure doesn't exist, but Jeb believes differently.

Why would John Ross return to Tennessee after their trip to Oklahoma? Jeb is sure that he left something valuable behind, and the Martyn Gale story corroborates the information that he has found.

The water splatters off the stone onto his wet pants. He leans forward touching the stone with his fingertips. "The faded T." He gasps as he traces the curved lines of the letter. His heart quickens, and he finds himself holding his breath. Jeb drops to his knees and rubs his fingers across a small thin line that encompasses the beautifully etched T. "This must be the door."

The thin line is parallel with the floor, as he examines the striations in the rock, he remembers Gale's words, "Behind the stone lies the message." Jeb takes a deep breath and removes a knife from his pocket. He slides the blade into the indentation above the "T." He licks his lips and slowly moves the knife horizontally, following the straight cut in the stone.

Sweat drips from his brow, making small round water stains on the smooth rock. He finds himself holding his breath as he nears the right angle where the horizontal line meets the vertical. The cut through the rock is perfectly smooth, like it was sawed with a diamond-tipped blade. How did someone in the early 1800s make such perfect cuts through solid rock?

He runs the blade along the entire perimeter of the square and finds that there isn't a triggering mechanism for the doorway.

"I guess I'm prying it open," he whispers. Jeb rubs his hands together and slowly grasps the knife.

He wiggles the knife backward and forward, causing the metal blade to bend. Jeb delicately extracts the blade and uses the tip to move the stone. Slowly, the square block moves outward. Puffs of dust drift upward as the block moves farther from the stone table.

Jeb grabs the base of the square rock and pulls it free with his right hand. A cold tepid air flows out from the void behind the block. He extends his hands into the darkness of the cavity. His fingers brush against a smooth object, and his heart jumps. A smile spreads across his face, and he quickly pulls a stained azure bottle from its enclosure.

The bottle is coated with a thin layer of yellow dust that rubs off on his hands. Jeb wipes the bottle clean and holds it up to his eye. Inside is a tightly rolled piece of paper with tears at the end. He examines the cork seal, and it appears to be completely intact. It looks like it has remained closed since Martyn Gale left it in the late 1800s.

Jeb holds the glass bottle in his left hand, rubbing the fingertips on his right hand together. He grabs the cork and delicately tugs the plug from the bottle. A puff of air escapes the opening that smells like the stagnant damp air in the cave. He slowly turns the bottle upside down, and the small roll of paper falls into his outstretched hand.

"What you got there?" Clem asks.

Jeb's eyes are bright, and he licks his dry lips repeatedly. "What we came for," Jeb says. The paper is coarse and brittle with small ornate letters drawn on the back of the page. He places the bottle in his pocket and gently unrolls the faded brown paper. As the paper unfurls, the lines of letters emerge along the top portion of the scroll and continue downward in paragraph form. The top paragraph is written in what appears to be Cherokee script.

"What does it say?" Clem questions.

Jeb glances to the right, and Clem is right beside him. He moves to the left a few steps, holding the paper delicately between his fingers. "This is the key to John Ross's stash."

"You didn't answer the question," Clem says.

"No, I can't, but I know someone who can."

Jeb gently rolls the scroll tightly and places it into the deep-blue bottle. He places the cork in the end and shoves it into his pocket.

"Now, let's get out of here," Jeb says, looking up at the high cavern walls. It should be easier getting out than getting in, and he is determined to stay dry this time.

Chapter 4

The Words of the Scroll

The breeze blows lightly across the smooth river, rustling the leaves on the tall oak trees growing along the grass-covered bank. White puffy clouds roll across the pale blue sky, riding on the soft invisible current. The afternoon drifts by lazily like the meandering flow of the river.

Jeb watches the bright white riverboat moving westward downstream on the Tennessee River, its zydeco music breaking the serenity of the lower part of the river. Jeb likes the old paddlewheel, but the music is something he can't get accustomed to. He puts on his water shoes and grabs his paddle. He looks forward to his river journey upstream toward the center of town and then a nice relaxing ride on the current back to the marina.

He throws his paddle into the compartment and climbs into his kayak bobbing on the wake beside his houseboat. Jeb likes to paddle the river when he needs to think, and today is one of those days. The scroll that he found in Georgia still hasn't revealed its secrets, and at this point he needs a paddle up the river to help him think through the problem. What was John Ross saying with the bit of parchment? How is it going to lead him to the gold that he left behind?

Jeb climbs into the kayak and unties the leash from his boat. The kayak slowly drifts from the houseboat toward the concrete pillars that support the deck of the marina. He pushes the paddle into the light green water and pulls against the current.

The boat emerges in the main channel of the river, and he feels the pull of the strong current downstream away from Camden. He pushes the oars deeper into the water and forces the small boat upstream. After fifteen minutes, the tall Victorian homes emerge around a slight bend of the river. They stand like sentinels along the riverfront, a throwback to the distant past.

Jeb churns through the water with droplets splashing from his oars onto his shirt. He nears the island that sits in the middle of the river. He will turn around here and catch the downstream current home.

He paddles the kayak close to the shore of the tree-covered island. The shadows from the tall trees shroud him in shadows. Small birds fly upward from the thick branches as he nears the muddy bank. The greenish water splashes against the bare land surface. Jeb takes a deep breath and opens his water bottle. He takes a few gulps and leans back in the seat. The white, puffy clouds drift across the sky, slowly changing into different shapes as they ride the currents aloft.

Jeb wipes his mouth with the back of his hand and throws the bottle into the compartment of the kayak. He takes his journal wrapped in plastic out of the hold and slowly opens the zip top. He opens the book with a red cord wrapped around the spine. He leans against the seat and stares at the artistically drawn letters that he copied from the walls of the cave..

He stares at it for a number of minutes, feeling the boat rise gently up and down on the current. Jeb runs his fingers through his brown hair and pushes his glasses further up the bridge of his nose. The longer he stares at it the more he realizes he is stuck deciphering the code. He called Dr. Wright immediately on his return from Georgia, but the professor had been away at a conference. Dr. Rhinehart told him it would be another week before Dr. Wright returned.

In the meantime, he had studied Cherokee script, but he was unable to break the code. Jeb also read and reread the Gale account continually, but it appears that Gale took the secrets to the hidden treasure with him. Martyn Gale left the clues to the cave where the blue gas was hidden, but that is all. Gale seems to appreciate the thrill of the hunt and wants the treasure hunters following in his footsteps to enjoy the journey.

Jeb closes the leather-bound book and touches the cool fabric to his lips. The water sloshes onto the dark brown bank causing his boat to tilt right and left. He thinks about the words that Gale had written. The treasure lies in a deep cave near Chattanooga, Tennessee. The geology of Tennessee is something that he knows a little about, and that causes a very big problem. Over seven thousand caves are near Chattanooga. Without an idea of where the treasure could be, that would be like finding a very tiny pin in one of those seven thousand caves in the dark.

The wind blows across the water, causing tiny ripples on the surface. The kayak rocks lightly on the small waves.

Jeb checks his watch and smiles. It is about time to pay Dr. Wright a visit. Jeb stows his book inside the kayak and grabs the paddle. He pushes off from the muddy bank and catches the river current south. It pulls him south along the busy downtown district. The lines of cars parked along the riverfront shine in the bright sunlight.

Jeb glances up at the iron bridge that spans the waterway. The commuters' car tires thump along the expansion joints of the bridge as they venture into town. Jeb spots a man looking down at him, following his path down river with what looks like a camera. He gives a wave and digs his paddle deeper into the water. With the force of his strokes and the speed of the current, he quickly leaves the bridge behind.

He glances over his shoulder, and the man's camera is still trained on him. Being the subject of a photographer is something new and he doesn't like it at all. He's not paranoid.

What do you want? Jeb thinks. His mind works frantically, trying to figure out what could be the reasons for all the attention. The guy didn't look like he belonged to the group that he had a run in with when he was hunting for Grant's lost treasure. Those guys were professionals, and they never would have let him see them.

This man is different. He wants to be seen, and that is what concerns Jeb. He paddles harder than he has ever paddled heading downstream. He wants to get to the houseboat so that he can head over to the university to see Dr. Wright, but Jeb also wants to get off the water where he is exposed. Being tailed is never a good thing, and he needs to be very careful.

Jeb steers the kayak into the marina and paddles toward his houseboat *The Kaiser's Redeemer*. Carl, his overprotective neighbor, leans against the railing.

"Getting a late start," Carl says.

"Sometimes I sleep in." Jeb smiles.

"Treasure hunting keeps you from working normal hours."

"Exactly."

Jeb throws the oar onto his boat, and the oar clatters across the deck. He grabs the rail and pulls the kayak alongside and quickly wraps the rope around the metal pole. With the bobbing kayak secure, Jeb climbs out of it.

"What do you have planned for the day?" Carl asks, leaning over the railing of his houseboat.

Jeb holds his journal in his hands and smiles. "Thought I would swing by the college for a bit."

"Ah. Lining up your next quest."

"Maybe."

"It involve that pretty lady?"

Jeb hadn't thought about Margaret in a few months, and it had been longer than that since she walked out his front door. He was a little relieved that he hadn't seen her. The search for U.S. Grant's gold shipment had not been an easy endeavor, and he almost died in the process.

"Not this time," Jeb replies, smiling.

"That's a pity. From what I saw, she was quite a woman."

Jeb would have to agree, but he was happy not having her in on his new venture.

"You be careful, son." Carl says.

Jeb nods and walks toward the front door. He grabs the knob and turns his head. Carl has that concerned look on his face. The one that a grandparent gives their grandkids when they don't approve of their life choices.

Jeb smiles. "Always." He opens the door and walks into the dark interior. Hopefully, this one will be different. Hopefully there won't be any other hair-raising events like he experienced in the cave.

*****

Bands of sunlight filter into the room through the blinds, forming small, yellow, rectangular shapes on the floor. A leather book lies on top of a crisply made bed with an ancient looking scroll beside it. The rough edges are browned and curled.

Jeb opens the bathroom door and walks toward the bed with his wet hair dripping onto his dark shirt. He pushes his glasses higher up onto his nose and retrieves the book and the scroll from the bed. The leather parchment feels rough and deeply textured in his fingers. He is sure that Dr. Wright's pale eyes will glitter excitedly when he sees this bit of history. He hopes that the professor will be able to shed some light on the meaning of the pictures drawn on the brittle leather.

He delicately places the journal and scroll into his bag and throws it over his shoulder. Time to go see the good doctor. Jeb walks toward the bedroom door, but he stops suddenly. What about that guy who was watching him from the bridge? What if he makes another appearance, but this time it is less about reconnaissance and more about interference? He turns and walks toward the bedside table. Jeb opens the drawer and grabs his thirty-eight. He can never be too careful.

He lowers the gun into his bag and closes the top, ready for anything or almost anything. Hopefully, this time things will go smoothly.

*****

The heat of the July afternoon in Camden is blistering. The leaves on the trees wilt in the blazing sunlight, and the grass along the roadway is brown and brittle. Camden, Tennessee, is a typical southern town that experiences excruciating long hot days in late summer. With very little rain, the oppressive heat mounts with each passing day.

Jeb steers his black Saab through the narrow streets around Montlake College. The exquisite Victorian homes line the roadway as he passes through the residential part of campus. These one-hundred-year-old houses are where most of the college professors live. The car zips up the hill, and he casually looks into his rearview mirror. Nothing. He presses the pedal farther to the floor, and the Saab speeds to the crest of the hill.

The campus spreads out ahead of him, and he turns right, slowing to match the thirty-five mile per hour speed limit. Students walk briskly, carrying their overpacked bookbags from one place to another. He makes another right and pulls into the parking lot of Holt Hall. The large brick building is the home of Montlake's history department.

A warm humid breeze blows through the open window, rustling the papers on the passenger seat. A vibrant-colored cardinal lands on the side mirror and moves its head up and down excitedly. The bird hops from the mirror to the dash chirping repeatedly. The hairs on the back of his neck stand on end as the bird continues flitting from the dash to the mirror.

Jeb chuckles. "What am I doing?". He grabs the journal, and the parchment from the seat and throws the door open. Closing the door, he looks back at the bird sitting motionless on the car. Its eyes remain fixated on him and the scroll.

"I'm going inside now," Jeb says, walking around the car. "When I come out, I expect you to be gone."

A few students walking along the sidewalk stare at him with quizzical looks. He doesn't look like a typical college student and he is thankful for that. Jeb smiles and hurries away from the gawking students and the cardinal that seems to have an unnatural interest in him. He takes the steps two at a time toward the large glass front door. Jeb takes a quick glance at the car, and the cardinal is still sitting on the side mirror staring at the glass door.

"I will deal with you later, bird," Jeb says, clutching the handle to the front door.

The welcoming cool air inside the building feels much better than the hot stagnant air outside. How did people in the south function before climate control? Ninety-five degrees with ninety percent humidity are never pleasant conditions, but it could be a modern phenomenon. When the Cherokee roamed these lands, there wasn't asphalt and concrete to radiate heat back into the air. The trees and grasses absorbed the energy from the sun and made the land more forgiving, more bearable.

Jeb hurries up the stairs and down the hallways toward Dr. Wright's office door. Jeb has spent more time in the buildings on campus since he graduated than he ever did while he was in school. He raps lightly on the wooden doorway, and immediately the coarse, husky voice of Dr. Wright answers, "Come in, Strauss."

He opens the door, and Dr. Wright is sitting at his desk with a pipe between his yellow teeth. Dr. Wright motions for him to sit, and Jeb walks across the office and sits. Dr. Wright's bright-green eyes dance. The professor is the most knowledgeable person concerning the history of Camden and the surrounding areas. His bookshelf is filled with historical interpretations that he has written.

"So, what do you have for me today?"

Jeb slides the rolled-up leather scroll across the polished desk. Dr. Wright's eyes narrow as he gazes down at the browned leather parchment.

"Late seventeen hundreds . . . early eighteen hundreds," he says, stroking his gray, pointed goatee.

"Eighteen hundreds, I believe," Jeb replies. "I hope anyway."

Dr. Wright delicately unrolls the parchment, and his eyes narrow the instant he sees the letters. His index finger traces the syllabary written on the leather scroll.

"You have a prize here," Dr. Wright says without taking his eyes from the page. "This is Sequoyah syllabary. A treasure in its own right." Dr. Wright looks up, his green eyes dancing. "Where did you find this?"

Jeb smiles. "Ah, a master never reveals his tricks."

"Well, if the master wants me to tell him what this says, then he should let me know where it was found."

"No need for that, Doc." Jeb laughs.

Jeb takes his journal from his pocket and opens it to the page where he has copied the glyphs from the cave.

"I found this hidden cavern near the Etowah River." Dr. Wright glances at the pictures traced on the page. "Where the river cuts through the ridge. A magical place. It's like the place where the river began."

"What do we have here?" Dr. Wright says, snatching the book and dragging it across the desk. His mouth moves silently as his finger glides across the page.

After a few minutes of Dr. Wright studying the scroll and the glyphs, Jeb decides to make his presence known. "Dr. Wright?"

Dr. Wright mutters to himself and strokes his gray goatee more vigorously.

Jeb stands and leans over the pages. "Can you read them?"

"I can read them, yes."

"What does it say?"

Dr. Wright places his pipe in its holder and scratches the side of his face. "These two accounts were written at different times." Dr. Wright points to the pictures in the journal. "These are the figures that the Cherokee used prior to Sequoyah, and in this prose, the writer describes the beginnings of the world and the birth of the people. It also tells of the great river that directs the paths of people."

That makes sense considering where the writing was found, but Jeb is more interested in what is written on the scroll. That is the piece of information that Martyn Gale left behind. What is on the scroll should lead to the John Ross treasure.

Dr. Wright looks up at Jeb, and his eyes aren't dancing like they were before. Jeb gets a sense that the professor is apprehensive. "I don't like that look on your face, Doc," Jeb finally says.

"The scroll was written much later. I would guess around 1830 or so judging by the tone."

"You mean prior to the Cherokee removal."

Dr. Wright nods his head slowly. "A horrible time for the people. Being betrayed by a government that they thought they could live peacefully with. Forced to march halfway across the country under grueling conditions."

Jeb has heard the stories of death along the Trail of Tears. The reality seems so barbaric and unnecessary. The lust for land in that age caused men to commit innumerable atrocities.

"It seems that the author of this text left something for when the people returned triumphantly to their ancestral home."

Jeb's pulse quickens. This is what he was looking for. There is a treasure, and it is hidden somewhere, and this bit of leather is the key to the riches.

"The elders hid the vast treasure of the people in a series of protected caverns."

"Protected?"

"Not sure if its physical or mystical protections, but in the text, it says that the horned beasts protect the entrance to the caverns."

"That doesn't sound good."

"I would say not."

Jeb places his hands on the desk and stares at the parchment. "Are you going looking for this?" Dr. Wright asks with concern in his voice. Jeb has never seen Dr. Wright act like this. Jeb glances at Dr. Wright.

Jeb nods his head slowly, certain that this is the right course to take. "Can you give me a transcription of this Sequoyah text?"

"I can," Dr. Wright replies. "But I will tell you that it is a series of journeys that end at the protected cavern. And at each leg, there are more clues that will lead to the next."

"You want to go on an expedition?" Jeb smiles. "Riches at the end of the rainbow."

"I'm too old for field work, Jeb. And I fear that this one will be dangerous."

"They're all dangerous."

"Sorry, Jeb."

"No problem, Doc. Get me the transcription."

"Will do."

Jeb moves the scroll and journal to his side of the desk.

"How can I transcribe without . . ." Dr. Wright asks.

"Your phone has a camera." Jeb replies.

"I'm going to need the originals." Dr. Wright takes his phone and takes a few pictures of the scroll and the pages in the journal.

Jeb rolls the parchment tightly together and places the journal in his pocket. "Thanks again, Doc."

"I will send the translation to you tomorrow. Email?"

Jeb nods. "That will work fine. Oh, can you send me a codex so I can translate the other clues when I get them."

"Sure."

Jeb turns and walks toward the door. He grips the handle, but before he can open the door, Dr. Wright's voice fills the room. "Be careful, Jeb."

Jeb opens the door. "Always am, Doc." Jeb closes the door behind him and hurries down the hallway, wondering what was written on the pages that spooked Dr. Wright.

CHAPTER 5

EAGLES TOWER

The morning air is already sticky with the humidity hovering at near ninety percent. The soft sounds of the tree frogs mingled with the cicadas creates a natural instrumental on the river at six in the morning. The waning full moon fades as the sun creeps closer to the eastern horizon.

Jeb stows his kayak on deck of the houseboat and tosses the oar inside the hold. He was up and ready this morning for the second leg of the journey to find the John Ross treasure. Doctor Wright sent over the translations and codex for the Sequoyah syllabary. The uneasiness he felt when he left Holt Hall has slowly lifted, but as he reads the words on the scroll, he needed a chance to think about what they meant.

The trip up the river on the kayak gave him the chance to organize his thoughts and set a plan of action for what comes next. The words written on the scroll are directions to the next marker. At some point, they lead to the end of the rainbow, but he doesn't have a clue to how many of these markers remain to be found.

Jeb sits on the deck chair and puts on his canvas cargo pants. The words on the scroll run through his mind as he slips on his boots.

The path of the buffalo ascends the steps of stone toward the pinnacle where the eagle rests. The water roars over the falls and shrouds the door of stone, but the eagle has left his mark and will lead the traveler onward.

The directions are straightforward, and he has contemplated the numerous possibilities of where this door of stone lies hidden. It has to be somewhere in the eastern portions of Tennessee. The mountains, plateaus, and ridges are perfect places where an object like this mark of the eagle could remain hidden for two hundred years. Just like the John Ross treasure, he believes the next clue is hidden inside a cave near the summit of one of these mountains.

Jeb walks inside and grabs his pack with the journal and scroll. He locks the front door and heads toward the landing. He strides up the gangway toward the marina parking lot. The other boats are quiet, and they roll softly on the wake of the river.

Jeb steps onto the gravel of the parking area. The crushed stone crunches under his feet, making a harsh abrasive sound under his boots. He scans the cars and the surroundings, looking for something that should not be there. A man with a camera watching his every move or a car following closely behind but fortunately no one is stirring this morning. He opens the door to the Saab and throws his pack in the passenger's seat. The cold metal of his thirty-eight presses into his back as he lowers himself into the driver's seat.

At the moment, all is calm and quiet, and that is the way he likes things. Jeb starts the car, and the engine roars to life. Orange, purple, and pink paint the sky to the east before the sun emerges over the ridges.

Jeb shifts the gears and presses the gas. Gravel spits out from under the tires, and a cloud of white smoke billows out behind the car like a thick river fog. The tires squeal as the car hits the asphalt, and he presses the gas away from the rising sun. The dark Saab races toward the blackness ahead just like the pathway to John Ross's treasure. It still remains in shadows.

Jeb has studied and read intensely about the Cherokee since Dr. Wright sent the translations. Knowing the location of the stair of stone and the pathway of the buffalo was imperative. Jeb taps the steering wheel as he races along Highway 41. His research led him to a decision. The Cumberland Plateau is a place where buffalo were present in the past. These large animals had to migrate from somewhere, and he thinks they moved from the flats of middle Tennessee eastward.

That would mean that the buffalo found a stairway up the rocky ridges toward the eagle's nest. The Cumberland Plateau is the western most promontory, and Jeb is certain that is where this stone doorway is located. That is the point of entry of the buffalo, and that is where he will find the next scroll.

The two-lane road is empty except for the Saab, and it speeds up to seventy miles an hour on the lonely roadway. Jeb glances into the rearview mirror and smiles. There isn't anything but vacant asphalt behind him. Maybe this time will be different from the others. Maybe this time there won't be any unwelcome guests or near-death experiences.

He passes over the old iron bridge that crosses the Tennessee River. The tires thump against the expansion joints that allow the bridge to expand and contract without failing. Another five minutes down the road and the highway ascends up the plateau.

Almost there, Jeb thinks, checking the rear view again.

*****

Jeb pulls the car into the Stone Door State Park parking lot. It is a busy place at nine in the morning with hikers and recreational walkers hitting the dirt path that leads to the Stone Door trailhead. An older couple with their little pug on a long leash stand beside the trail holding a map. Jeb parks the car and watches all the people through the windows and mirror. His heart starts beating faster like it knows something is about to happen. Jeb smiles. It always happens this way. Anytime he is out, the excitement of finding something causes his pulse to quicken and his heart to race.

He checks his watch. Nine fifteen. "Time to get going," he says. He throws the door open and a dry warm breeze rushes into the car. It's going to be one of those days. Being up in the ridges, he hopes the weather will be a little cooler, but even fourteen hundred feet on the Plateau isn't enough height to escape the heat and humidity.

Jeb steps out of the car, grabs his pack, and throws it over his shoulder. He looks like a hardcore hiker without the walking poles. Jeb slips his Ray-Bans on and heads toward the dirt path leading to the beginning of the trail.

The path is made of hard-packed clay, and it goes along a horizontal grade for roughly three hundred feet turning into a narrower turning passage that meanders through the old growth oak and pine. The trail dips and angles upward toward a small knoll. A few hikers walk down the path toward him.

"How's the trip?" Jeb asks.

"Going down is easy." The tall hiker replies.

"Coming up, not so much." The female hiker adds.

"Thanks for the info." Jeb smiles.

After walking another ten minutes, the trees thin, and the trail transforms from dirt to brownish-orange stone. He has reached the sandstone cap rock of the plateau where fractures in the rock have made the huge slabs appear like giant checkerboard. He stands at the edge of the rocky trail looking out at the gorge and the valley below. He can see for miles through the pass between the ridges to the valley. A small river meanders out into the plain bordered by green foliage.

The entire gorge is covered by a thick green canopy, and the leaves wave at him as the breeze blows through the pass. The eagle's nest is somewhere on this ridge, and he plans on finding it. Jeb pulls the straps on his pack tight and steps on the uneven rocks along the cliff. One wrong move on this treacherous part of the trail, and he would plummet a few hundred feet onto hard rocks.

He places his feet carefully on the weathered stones, and some shift under his feet. At the apex of the ridge, the trail quickly descends through a narrow passage between the vertical columns of rock. It looks like a stairway built for giants with large slabs of rock forming the steps.

The passage is empty and hidden from the morning sun. Jeb creeps downward slowly, looking up at the sheer faces of the rock hidden in the shadows. This has to be the path the buffalo took to the top of the plateau. Where is the nest? He scans the rocks, searching for a drawing or an indentation or a cavern where the eagle could hide.

Halfway down the stairway, an intersection pathway bisects the stairway and curves around a tall pillar of rock that is almost spherical. Jeb's heart jumps in his chest. He runs down the stairs and climbs over a large boulder onto a sandy narrow ledge that curves around the giant formation. Jeb looks up at the vertical column of sandstone, and the small tufts of grass and roots of the trees extend out over the cap stones. It looks like a nest. A circular nest. Just like an eagle, and this rock structure is cut off from the others.

Jeb glances behind him, but this side of the formation is hidden from the stairway. "Let's get to it," he says.

He lowers his pack and pulls out a pair of climbing shoes. Jeb slips them on and looks up the rock column where he spots a cavity in the rock. He steps backward, and there below the summit is a small opening in the sandstone.

"A good place to hide something." Jeb says.

He rubs his fingers together and licks his lips repeatedly. Small protrusions of stone from the rock face will give him hands holds and foot holds. Jeb claps his hands together and reaches to grasp the first rectangular rock. It is coarse like sandpaper, scratching into his skin as he pulls himself upward.

Pulling his body higher up the formation, Jeb looks down at the ground. He is twenty feet above the small sandy pathway where he began his climb. His biceps and triceps burn, and his fingers are dry and sore. He takes a few deep breaths and looks up at the cavity in the rock. It is still twenty feet above him.

"Maybe I should have brought some rope," he says, hugging the wall.

A swift dry wind blows from the valley up the gorge and whirls around the circular outcrop. His shirt whips back and forth, and he grips the rock tightly with his aching fingers, but the wind pushes his body away from the rock face. "Can't stay here," he says.

He scurries rectangular rock to rectangular rock up another ten feet. The wind whips his hair and sends bits of sand into his eyes. He blinks repeatedly, trying to get the abrasive grains out of his eyes, but the scratchy particles rub against the edges of his eyes causing his vision to blur.

Jeb wants to wipe the tears and loosen material from his eyes, but that would mean falling thirty feet onto the rocks. He grits his teeth and narrows his eyes. Looking up through the falling sediment, he grasps another hand hold and pulls himself higher. Before he can set his feet, a violent wind roars around the eagle's nest. He grips the rock with all of his strength as his feet dangle.

Jeb struggles to find a place for his feet. He swings from right to left, and his finger slip on the sandstone tearing small lines in his skin. Looking for a foothold, he looks downward and with a sickening dizziness the rocks swim below him. His feet brush against smooth stone.

"I'm not going out like this," Jeb growls. Through the searing pain in his eyes, he focuses on the rocks near his feet. A small rock protrudes about an inch from the main body, and he quickly lifts his leg and places his foot on the stone. He pushes with his weary legs and pulls his body upward with his bloody fingers.

He finds a place for his other foot and looks upward. The cave is right above him. He claws and pulls through the wild current of air until he rolls his body into the dark cave. The ceiling is smooth with tiny droplets of water clinging to the exposed rock. Jeb coughs loudly, and the sound echoes through the chamber. It must be much larger than it looks because the sound continues resonating downward through the tall column of rock.

Jeb strains his tired muscles to regain a sitting position. His entire body aches from the exertion used during the climb. He takes a few deep breaths and peers out the opening. The view from this eagle's nest is breathtaking. This vantage point gives a perfect view of the gorges below and the white cascading waterfall far north of the cave. The trail up the passage can be seen from where it begins along the stream in the valley all the way up the stone stairs.

This is a well-positioned palisade to monitor the comings and goings along the trail. How long had it been used by the natives? Jeb takes a small tactical flashlight out of his pocket and backs away from the opening shining the bright yellow light against the stone. The light moves from one side of the cavern to the other, chasing the shadows from the enclosure. The cave is more like a small circular room with a depression in the center tainted with black soot. He runs his fingers across the black rock and small streaks of black transfer to his hand. Small circular holes sit on opposite sides of the depression.

"An ancient fire pit, complete with a place for your barbeque poles."

Jeb moves farther into the room, and the light hits the back wall. Three lines of characters appear faded on the cold brownish-orange stone. He places the flashlight in his mouth and retrieves his journal from his pocket.

Staring at a paragraph, he removes the pencil from the book and turns the pages.

Holding the book up to the letters etched on the wall, he slowly transcribes the letters into his journal. Small drops of water sprinkle onto the brown pages from the ceiling five feet above him. He wipes the beads of water from the pages and continues copying the text. The dripping water slaps against the stone beside him, and a faint trickling sound catches his attention.

He places the pencil inside the book and removes the light from his mouth. "I'll translate you later."

The beam of light moves across the floor, and a small stream of water the width of his pencil flows behind him. The tinkling sound grows louder as he crawls along the floor, following the small stream. The stream disappears at the base of the opposite wall. Jeb shines his light into the manhole-sized opening in the floor. The water droplets collide with the hard rock, creating a mist of smaller drops.

His yellow beam of light never hits the bottom. Jeb trains the light on the edges of the spherical hole in the solid stone, and a long shadow moves from the top lip of the opening downward. He slithers across the smooth rock and reaches into the depression. His fingers brush against the coarse material that feels like banded cords of hemp on his scratched fingertips.

The thick rope disappears into the darkness beyond the flashlight beam. Jeb takes a deep breath. "I guess I should go down there and see what lies hidden in the darkness."

He studies the rope intently questioning how long it had been here. Did the natives place it here or did some kids from the mountain do it? Jeb pulls on the rope, and it is firmly embedded in the smooth, circular rock.

The circular tunnel is almost perfectly smooth. No footholds or places for his hands. The rope is the only way down. It will be like rappelling, something that Jeb doesn't mind doing. It is much easier going down than climbing up.

"Well, no better time than now," he says. He sets the flashlight between his teeth carefully dangles his legs over the edge. He gives the rope one final strong pull, and it remains securely attached to the rock wall. This is the only part of the treasure-hunting career that can be a bit nerve wracking, hoping that a two-hundred-year-old piece of rope will hold his weight.

Chapter 8

Bottom of the Well

Jeb takes a deep breath and slowly swings over the edge. The rough cord digs into his skin, opening the small lacerations at the fingertips. Blood trickles onto the rope, making it appear much darker than it is already. Jeb grips the flashlight between his teeth and looks down into the darkness of the deep well. The faint light is swallowed by the blackness exactly like the sunlight is consumed by the darkness in a deep water well.

With his feet braced against the smooth rock, he slowly descends into the chasm of blackness. The rope holds firm all the way to the bottom. Jeb steps onto a gray undulating rock surface that is wet with the water from above. He has to be at the base of the eagle's nest where he started earlier in the day.

He shines the light on the smooth walls and sees glyphs and elaborate drawings etched on all the surfaces. The clue has to be written in the artwork on the cave wall. With his heart beating wildly, Jeb takes his journal from his pocket and opens it to where his pencil marks the page. Delicately, he traces the letters and drawings into the book, moving his pencil lightly across the pages.

His eyes dart from page to rock wall, and he studies the figures and letters making sure that they have been transcribed perfectly. After ten minutes of careful and accurate copying, Jeb leans against the wall and removes the translations from Dr. Wright. "Let's find out what you're hiding."

With each letter and glyph, he begins the process of deciphering the clue. "F . . . I . . . R . . . E . . ."

Jeb taps the page with the end of his pencil and continues with the translation. Small beads of sweat form on his brow and they trickle down his face.

"S . . . H . . . I . . . N... . . . E . . . I . . . N . . . T . . . O . . . " He scribbles the next part of the message onto the paper. As he stares at the words, a faint sound like something metal tapping against a rock drifts down from somewhere above him.

He looks up from the paper and listens more intently. The tapping starts and stops abruptly. He shines the light upward toward the eagle's nest, but the light only makes it a few feet. Stone door is a place where rock climbers like to go because of the near vertical faces. Jeb holds his breath and listens for any other sounds.

After a few moments without the sound's return, Jeb laughs. "A bit paranoid today," he says. He points the beam at the page and begins again with the next line of the clue. "T . . . H . . . E . . . V . . . A . . . L . . . Small bits of dust float in the air around the bright light from his lamp. "L . . . E . . ."

The light tapping begins again and the rain of dust intensifies. Jeb shines the light upward, and the rope sways slightly as if it is caught in a soft breeze.

Jeb shoves the book in his pocket and circles the bottom of the well. His mouth is dry, and sweat pours from his brow.

"There is someone up there," he whispers. "They're trying to work the rope free." He retrieves the revolver from his belt and points it upward into the darkness.

A thought comes into his mind quickly. *What if whoever is up there has a gun? I am in a barrel. An easy target with no place to go.* All the possibilities that lie ahead of him are unappealing, but he has to do something.

He grips the handle of his thirty-eight and holds his breath. His fingers press against the cold metal of the trigger, and he pulls. Fire erupts out of the end of the barrel, and he hears the muffled scuttling of feet far above him.

"That was unwise," a harsh voice yells from the eagle's nest.

Jeb turns the light off and presses himself against the wall trying to be as small as possible. He dares not speak, and he breathes slowly, hoping that will not give away his position.

"You are not welcome here, Mr. Strauss."

Well, this person knows who he is, and it could be the same guy from the bridge.

"We cannot allow you to succeed in your quest. You threaten to destroy the heritage of the people, and we cannot allow that to happen."

"How about you let me come up that rope, and we can talk about it?" Jeb yells.

"You shot at us, Mr. Strauss. It is much better that you remain where you are."

Jeb thinks about emptying the other chambers into the darkness. He might hit one of them this time. The thought of being struck by a ricocheting bullet doesn't even register.

"You are in a bad position, Mr. Strauss, but we are a reasonable people."

"Yeah. How is that?" Jeb replies.

"We could shoot you with ease, but we will not do that."

"How nice of you," Jeb says.

"You speak in such an insolent tone. You are nothing more than a thief, and you will be repaid for your greed."

"How about you let me out of here, and we can talk things out face to face?"

"Unfortunately for you, you will remain where the treasures you seek shall remain. Hidden."

The rope falls with a thud, coiling up in a large pile at the bottom of the well. Jeb shines his flashlight on the bunched cord.

"That's not good," Jeb whispers. "Hey! You can't leave me down here!"

"Good day, Mr. Strauss," the voice says.

The sound of boots on exposed stone drifts down to the bottom of the well.

"HEY. GET ME OUT OF HERE!" The words echo around the circular room until the bouncing vibrations dissipate into nothingness.

Well, this is a first, Jeb thinks, circling the round enclosure and pushing against the solid stone. The rock doesn't budge. He continues pressing his back against the smooth rock every five feet. Again and again, the rock remains stationary.

Jeb falls to the ground with sweat pouring down his face. Resting his head against the rock, he moves the beam of the flashlight up the rock face where the rope was fastened.

"I guess I could climb out." Jeb breathes slowly. "There have to be divots from where the rope was secured." His mind calmly focuses on the manner in which that rope had remained embedded in the stone all those years.

What kind of anchor did they use? It should still be attached to the rope. Jeb hops to his feet and walks across the circular room to the pile of rope coiled up on the floor. He runs the length of rope through his hands, straightening it out behind him. Finally, he holds the end and attached to the strong cord is a piece of copper with a wheel on the end that looks like a small gear. Dust from the sandstone clings to the strong metal.

"Well, that solves that mystery," Jeb says, staring up at the smooth rock above. "Quite ingenious use of metals by the natives, but it's not going to help me out of this hole." He looks upward, and small drops of water shower down upon him.

His heart jumps. All that water from the top is going somewhere. Jeb falls to the ground and crawls along the floor on his hands and knees. A smile spreads across his face. The small channel of water flows along the floor and disappears into a small circular depression at the base of the wall. He hadn't noticed the small sliver light visible between the wall and the floor.

"The way out." Jeb presses his body to the floor and looks through the crack. The dusty trail is on the other side of this thin piece of stone. He rolls onto his back and places his feet against the smooth rock. *Whack. Whack.* The heels of his shoes smash against the stone again and again. A small linear crack appears on the sandstone from the floor to the next slab above.

He braces himself against the floor and strikes the rock again. *Whack. Whack. Whack. Thunk.* Jeb's foot goes through, and bright sunlight flows into the well. He pulls his foot through the hole and crawls to the opening. It is a foot wide and a foot high and is a bit small for a grown man's body.

"I need a little more space," Jeb says. He kicks at the crumbling rock, and clouds of smoke billow around the opening. Another chunk of rock from the wall flies into the dusty path.

"Hey!" a woman's voice says. "Is someone in there?"

Jeb coughs. "Yeah. I just got a little lost and ended up down here."

"Can we help you?"

Jeb looks out of the hole and kneeling beside the opening are three woman wearing hiking shorts and tank tops.

The brunette holds out her hand. "How did you end up in there?" Her bright green eyes sparkle in the bright sunlight.

"That is a funny story indeed," Jeb replies. "And I will tell you all about it if you can help me out of here. But before we do that. Are there any other people around?"

"Just us," she replies.

"Oh, good. Then let's get me out of here."

A sense of relief flows through Jeb. The guys that trapped him in the rock prison have left, and a nice turn of events has occurred, being rescued by three college-age day trippers.

"All right. Grab my arms and pull," Jeb says, extending his arms through the opening.

Three sets of soft hands grab his scratched and sore arms and slowly pull him through the narrow passage. The broken rock scrapes against his skin, sending fresh jolts of pain coursing through him. His head emerges with torso following slowly behind.

"That's good," Jeb says.

He looks up at the three women huddled around him staring in bewilderment. "Are you hurt?" the woman with short blond hair asks.

"No, I'm good. I'm just going to lie here a minute."

"What were you doing in there?"

Jeb laughs. "I am doing a field study on Native American cave drawings. It is a fascinating subject. Unfortunately, my colleagues thought it would be good fun to remove my rope."

"Were those the others you were asking about?"

"The very ones."

"It is probably good they aren't here, huh?" the blonde says. "I know if it were me, I would push them off the ledge."

He slowly climbs to his feet, and dust and rock drops to the ground around his feet. "I cannot thank you three enough for pulling me out of there. I'm Jeb, by the way. Jeb Strauss."

The brunette holds out her hand. "I'm Madelyn. This is Josy," she says, pointing to the blonde.

The quiet dark-haired woman with dark brown eyes smiles. "I'm Celeste."

Jeb brushes his shirt and pants, sending plumes of dust into the air. "It must be fate that sent you my way today." Jeb laughs.

"Have you finished with your work?" Celeste asks.

"Yes." He pats his field book. "Everything is in here."

"We are going to stop by the Cape when we get to the top," Celeste says.

"And we would love for you to join us," Josy says.

"We would love to hear all about Native American cave drawings," Madelyn finishes.

Jeb looks at each of them. He could grab his bag and do the sensible thing and go back to *The Kaiser* and figure out the next clue. He coughs. "That sounds like a wonderful plan. I am a little parched."

"Wonderful," Madelyn says, squeezing his arm.

He looks down at her hand resting on his arm. He deserves a little break after all. The riddle will be there tomorrow, but Celeste, Josy, and Madelyn probably won't be. Jeb grabs his pack from the bushes around the eagle's nest and follows the three women up the stairs of the buffalo.

CHAPTER 9

WHERE IS THE SUN?

The houseboat rocks lightly on the wake from a passing barge carrying gravel and sand downriver. The water splashes against the hull with each rise and fall of the boat. Across the river, the morning log jam of cars making the trek into Camden begins. Jeb sits on a deck chair with his journal laid open on the table. He gazes at the stream of brake lights and is thankful that he doesn't work downtown. The engineering position he turned down would have him moving in that repetitious line every morning for the next thirty years.

A broad smile spreads across his face. He looks at his journal and the bold letters that he carefully wrote on the page.

The Sun Makes Fire That Shines Into The Valley. From This Rock, Our Fathers Have Watched Our People Grow Into A Powerful Nation And This Rock Will Reveal The Fortunes of Our People.

Jeb grabs his glasses and places the end into his mouth. Where is this rock? That is the question that has occupied his mind for the past week. That and who the guys were who tried to entomb him at Stone Door? He hadn't made much headway in answering either question. He had thought about going to see Dr. Wright again, but he didn't want to endanger the professor if they were watching him.

Those guys probably think he was still at the bottom of the well, and he wants to keep it that way for the moment. He will solve this riddle on his own with a little bit of legwork, but that has been fruitless so far.

"Morning, Jeb," Carl says.

Jeb turns and waves. Carl leans over the wooden railing of his houseboat, studying him. "You had quite a full house last night."

"Just a few friends."

"From where I was sitting, it looked like they were all female friends."

Jeb laughs. "The get together didn't disturb you. did it?"

"No. But I do wish you would have invited me over. I do like a good party."

"Next time." Jeb smiles. "Come on over, Carl."

Jeb pushes the other seat around the table out, and Carl slowly descends the stairs from his deck and climbs up onto *The Kaiser*. He sits keeping his eyes on the water ahead of them.

"They have something to do with whatever you're working on now?" Carl asks.

Jeb pushes the journal toward the old man. "Yeah, they just happened to be in the right place at the right time."

Jeb had spent the afternoon of his rescue with Madelyn, Josy, and Celeste. They were all juniors at the University of the South. They talked about economics, engineering, archaeology, and business. He hadn't had that kind of effortless conversation since Fran left for Costa Rica, and he hadn't realized how much he missed it. They spent most of their college years together, and his plan was to marry her. Unfortunately, Fran moved before he could ask her, and he didn't want to be the reason she stayed in Camden.

All three of them had been intrigued by what he was doing with his life. They never had met a real-life treasure hunter. Jeb got the sense that they were more attracted to the excitement of the chase more than anything. Like a living Indiana Jones movie. He invited them out to his boat as a thank you for saving his life, and last night, they all came over. Jeb prepared a fine spread of grilled shrimp and lobster followed by stories from the field.

"As your friend, I just ask for some consideration next time. There will be a next time?"

"You're on the guest list, but we do stay up late. It might be more than you can handle."

Carl's eyes narrow and he glares at him. Jeb laughs. "You're more man than I will ever be, Carl. Your stories about Vietnam and all the side projects you had over there would be more thrilling than anything I can talk about. I think the ladies would be captivated by them."

The old man smiles, and his eyes dance as if he remembers some of his former exploits. He looks down at the journal. "What does this mean?" Carl asks.

"That is the million-dollar question," Jeb replies, placing his glasses on the bridge of his nose. The prospect of finding John Ross's treasure swims before him like a shining sun, but this part of the riddle is a little harder to crack. What place where the sun lights the valley could it be talking about? The Cherokee lived in valleys all over East Tennessee, and that made finding it much more difficult.

"What kind of treasure is it?"

Jeb stares out at the slow-moving water of the Tennessee River. Part of Cherokee life is found along this river. "The John Ross treasure," Jeb replies.

"Never heard of that one."

"Most people think it's a myth, but I found this old account from a man named Martyn Gale."

"Never heard of him either."

"The newspaper did an article on him back in 1887," Jeb says, pulling a small paper clipping from the journal. Carl takes the yellowed paper from his hands and reads.

"Martyn Gale supposedly discovered that John Ross hid large amounts of gold and silver before he ever went west to Oklahoma," Jeb says.

Carl looks up from the paper. "You think it's real."

"John Ross came back to the area for something, didn't he?"

"And this is a clue to the treasure?"

"That's the part I'm working on."

Watching Jeb, Carl leans back in the chair with his fingers clasped behind his head. Jeb looks at the green ridges that surround the river.

After a few minutes of silence, Carl leans forward. "There isn't any danger with this one?" he asks with grandfatherly concern.

Jeb keeps his eyes on the rolling hills. "Not a bit."

Carl pushes away from the table and walks toward the railing. "Next time there's a party, don't forget me," Carl says.

"You're first on the guest list."

Carl climbs down the stairs and walks along the gangway toward his boat. Jeb knows that he is always concerned about him. Whether it is his choice in career or his prospects of a family in the future, Carl genuinely cares. Jeb can't say the same for his real family.

Chapter 10

At the Cabana

A few more days of fruitless research sitting at his computer searching for anything that would lead him to the Rock of the Fathers makes the three day headache much worse. Jeb yawns loudly and rubs the bridge of his nose. The glow from the computer screen lights up the houseboat's interior. He closes his laptop and sits in the darkness listening to the tick of the clock as the seconds drift slowly by never to return.

It is nine thirty, and the faint chirping of the frogs serenades him, making him sleepier with each passing second.

"That is enough for today," Jeb says, standing. He strides across the room and draws the curtain to the side. The American flag on the boat sways lightly in the warm evening river breeze.

The river is dark with small specks of light reflecting off the surface creating a kaleidoscope effect on the water. He finds the river at night to be relaxing, and sometimes he sits out on deck until the early morning hours thinking. He finds that the deck of his boat is where he does his best work, but tonight he needs sleep.

Jeb closes the curtain and treads toward the bedroom. He can already feel the soft, fluffy mattress under his tired body. A low-volume buzzing breaks through the sound of the chirping frogs. The light from the mobile phone shines brightly on the table, illuminating the journal and the closed computer.

Receiving phone calls this late at night is unusual for Jeb. There aren't that many people who have his number. Jeb taps his fingers on the door handle, contemplating letting it go to voicemail. He shakes his head and walks toward the table. Looking down at the number, he grabs the phone.

"Hey, Madelyn," Jeb says. "Hope everything is all right?"

"I just thought I would let you know that I would be… well me and Celeste will… We will be heading down to Camden tomorrow, and we wanted to know if you wanted to meet up someplace."

Jeb closes his eyes. That might put him another day behind on his John Ross project, and he doesn't want to neglect his work. "I don't think I will be able to make it tomorrow," he replies.

"You're sounding like one of those all work and no social life stick in the muds," she responds.

"It would probably be a lot of fun. I know."

"You're right about that," Madelyn says.

He rubs his eyes and yawns. "And I might have some information for you," she continues.

Jeb remains silent, thinking about what information she could have. He had told them about the cave drawings and the interpretations of the syllabary. They had been fascinated by the wording and hidden beauty of the words.

"I found some information about those cave writings, and I thought you might find it interesting," Madelyn says.

With his curiosity heightened, Jeb runs his fingers through his hair. "You could tell me now," he says.

"That isn't fun," she replies. "This gives us all a chance to hang out."

"All right."

"It is settled. We will drop by your place at eight. That isn't too late for a working stiff, is it?"

"See you then."

"Can't wait," Madelyn replies. "See you tomorrow."

With a click, the phone darkens. He tosses it on the couch and walks toward the bedroom. What information could she get that he couldn't? Who has she told about what he is looking for? Has word gotten out to the men that left him stranded in the well? The questions mount without an answer to any of them.

Jeb falls onto his feathery comfortable bed and stares at the ceiling. The tiredness has passed and a flurry of thoughts fill his overactive mind.

"Why did you answer the phone?" Jeb says to the darkness.

*****

The sweltering afternoon slowly drifts toward evening like the greenish brown water that drifts under the boat. The pink, purple, and red color from the setting sun paints the sky in distinctive lines that exhibit the wonderment found in creation's beauty.

Jeb pulls on his loafers and watches the paddleboarders enjoying a fantastic Camden sunset on the water. The sound of tires on gravel draws his attention, and he turns his head in the direction of the parking lot. A black Mercedes fills the space beside his Saab. *They are punctual,* he thinks, getting to his feet. He jumps onto the gangway and strides toward the lot.

"You ready?" Madelyn yells through the open window of the car. Her bright green eyes sparkle like fresh cut emeralds.

"Yeah. Yeah." Jeb smiles. "Where we heading this evening?"

"It's a surprise."

Jeb grabs the handle to his car, but Madelyn shakes her head. "You're riding with us. I bet I'm a better driver than you," she says with her lip curling into a smile.

Riding in the back seat and being chauffeured around Camden isn't what Jeb envisioned for this evening. He also likes knowing where he is going.

"You've got it all planned?" Jeb says.

Madelyn's eyes dance and her smile grows wider. "I'm good at being in control."

Jeb opens the back door and climbs into the seat.

"Hey, Jeb," Celeste says from the passenger seat, smiling. "I would listen to her."

Before he can fasten his seatbelt, Celeste turns the volume up on the radio where some 1990s grunge rock song blares loudly. They laugh wildly. Madelyn presses the gas, and the car speeds out of the parking lot, sending bits of gravel flying. Clouds of dust billow out behind the car. Jeb closes his eyes and taps his fingers against his thigh, hoping for a safe trip to wherever they are going.

*****

After fifteen tense minutes—minutes that seemed to extend for far too long—the car comes to a stop. Jeb opens his eyes slowly, and Madelyn and Celeste are staring at him.

"I thought you like adventure?" Madelyn says with her eyes narrowed questioningly.

Jeb smiles. "I do, but I don't know if this would qualify. Riding back here resembled imminent death and dismemberment."

Jeb opens the door and quickly gets out of the backseat. Stationary ground has never felt more wonderful. Madelyn opens the door and looks up at him, holding her hand out for him to take. Performing his chivalrous duty, he grasps her hand and helps her from the seat. Madelyn stands close to him, and the smell of lavender and cream mingles with her every breath.

"My driving scares you?"

"Maybe a bit, and that is saying something because I'm not easily frightened."

"That is good. Real good." Madelyn smiles.

Celeste walks around the car shaking her head. "I could have stayed at home and left this for the two of you." She loops her arm around Madelyn's and pulls her toward the door. They watch him as they near the white stucco building with tall banana trees swaying near the front entrance.

"What am I doing?" Jeb whispers, following them.

The bright neon lights of The Last Cabana flash like they belong on the Strip in Las Vegas, showering the street with endless jets of purple and red light. Jeb has been to the club that plays Caribbean-style music and serves tall fruity drinks topped with multiple umbrellas a few times before. The crowds are always festive, and the fresh mahi-mahi mixed with plantains make for an enjoyable evening.

Jeb hurries to catch up with his two companions, and the steel drum greets his ears as the door swings open. Somehow the smell of the ocean fills the room, and he isn't sure if the aromas of the islands are pumped into the room or if the saltiness and coconut in the air is authentic.

Madelyn and Celeste maneuver through the crowded dance floor toward the elevated round tables that line the sunken dance area. Jeb zigs and zags around swaying couples performing their best rumbas. Dancing was something that he never did, but he always found that people that knew what they were doing could make the music more real. A fast-moving couple spins in front of him, and he dodges them.

Madelyn grabs his hand and leads him up the stairs toward the tables. "You will join me later!" she yells over the music, pointing toward the floor.

"Of course," he lies.

Celeste is already seated and talking to an abnormally tan waiter with bright white teeth.

"I thought we had lost you," Madelyn says, squeezing Jeb's hand tightly.

"In a place like this, it is easy to do."

Jeb sits beside Madelyn, and Bright Teeth saunters over to him. "What can I get for you, sir?"

"Something without an umbrella," Jeb says.

"Make that two," Madelyn says. "I like a bit of adventure too."

The waiter nods and walks away. The music isn't as loud in the elevated dining section of the club, and that is refreshing. This isn't the music that Jeb usually enjoys. He would prefer being at Fitzhume's listening to big band music. There is nothing better than Julian Day and his trombone performing Glen Miller.

"I ordered us some coconut shrimp," Celeste says from across the table.

"That sounds good," Jeb replies.

Celeste leans forward in her chair. "Have you had any luck with the cave drawings you were studying?"

Jeb glances from Celeste to Madelyn. "At the moment, I am at a standstill."

Madelyn's green eyes dance in the bright lights, and her mouth twitches like she is trying to keep a smile from forming. That is why he is here after all to get the information that she has, and it seems that she hasn't told Celeste about it.

"That is unfortunate," Celeste says. "I was hoping for another daring story about how you found some obscure artifact that led you to some hidden treasure. A *National Treasure* type of tale."

Madelyn places her hand on his arm and grasps it lightly. "They never seem to work out like a Nicholas Cage movie."

Jeb smiles. The waiter returns with a tray with two tumblers filled with a dark liquid with ice and no umbrellas and a large sink type container filled with a coconut-smelling ice with four tall umbrellas protruding from the top.

"Thanks," Jeb says, taking the small tumbler from the tray. He passes the dark brown liquid to Madelyn and removes the other glass from the tray.

She takes a sip, and her nose scrunches. "This is not fruity."

"No umbrellas," Jeb replies.

"This is fruity, and it tastes so good."

"This is not," Madelyn says. "I don't know how anyone could drink something this bad?"

Jeb drains his glass in one gulp and sets it on the wooden table. He looks at Madelyn and smiles. "So, what information do you have for me?"

She swirls the liquid in her glass keeping her eyes fixed on him. She lifts the glass to her lips without dropping her gaze and turns the glass up. The liquid inside is gone instantly, and she places the glass on the table beside his.

"Later." She smiles. "Let's have some fun before we muddle it with business."

The waiter drops two fresh glasses of the aged rum at their table, and Jeb picks up his glass. "To fun," he says, and he touches his glass to both of theirs.

Time drifts by slowly as the three friends talk about travel, food, and music. The grilled mahi-mahi tastes terrific, and Jeb sits back in his chair finishing his drink. The low hum of the steel drum mixed with the strumming guitar makes him feel like he is at a resort on an island somewhere far from Camden. Far from the failures of searching for the John Ross treasure. This little night out has done him some good after all. The girls laugh and sing along with the music.

"I wish I had a pencil thin mustache . . ." Jeb chuckles at their off-key performance and downs the final drops of what is left in his glass and places it on the table.

The music ends, and loud applause and whistles fill the room.

"Thank you," the band leader says. "We hope you enjoy this one." The music starts, and it is much slower with a smooth drum line.

Madelyn grabs Jeb's hand, pulling him to his feet. "I said later."

"I don't dance," Jeb replies.

"You do tonight," Madelyn says.

She walks toward the stairs pulling him behind her. "I will wait here." Celeste says.

Jeb turns shrugging his shoulders. This isn't something that appeals to him. He is a listen-to-the-music type of a person, not an active participant in the rhythms and melodies.

Madelyn glances back and gives him a half smile and her bright eyes flash in the dazzling lights. Jeb follows without thinking about his two left feet getting in the way. He smiles watching her body move to the sound of the music and hearing her laughter as they get closer to the dance floor.

The dancers on the floor move perfectly to the beat, swaying to the beat of the steel drum. Madelyn lifts his arm high in the air and spins under it, grazing his arm with the top of her head. Her eyes never leave his as she moves toward him like she is floating across the floor on a cloud. The smell of lavender and cream drifts into his nose as she pulls in close to his body. Her green eyes are hypnotic like the Caribbean waters where the music is played.

"Relax," Madelyn says.

"Not much of a dancer."

"Watch my body move. I know you like to," Madelyn says.

Jeb laughs, looking away toward the band. She grabs his waist and pulls him into a close embrace, moving her hips right and left against him. Her sweet aroma drifts around him, floating effortlessly like the feet of the dancers on the floor.

Madelyn slowly moves her right hand from his waist, and it grazes his arm before she places her hand in his. She smiles at him, and Jeb laughs and moves his body slowly.

"That's it." Madelyn laughs.

Jeb moves then around the dance floor, doing his best not to step on her feet. He has seen enough ballroom dancing at Fitzhume's, and he tries to move his feet like the dancers do there.

"You're not too bad," Madelyn says cheerfully. "And you're relaxing, finally."

"Not bad for a first timer."

"A natural." She smiles.

He slowly forgets about his inability to dance and simply enjoys the time, moving along the dance floor to the melodic music. This night out has done something for him. It has taken him away from the frustrations of the John Ross treasure. He isn't worried about being stumped, or worried about the men who tried to kill him. Maybe that is what Madelyn is trying to do. Take him away from the worries, and simply have fun for an evening, and that is something that he hasn't allowed since Fran left two years ago. Jeb has been all business since then, living like a hermit focused on unearthing lost treasure.

One slow song leads into another, and they glide around the room, spinning slowly. He touches her face lightly and moves a few strands of hair that have fallen over her eyes.

"Thanks for the evening," he says softly.

"At least, there is a prize at the end," Madelyn says.

"What would that be?"

"Don't act like you have forgotten. The only reason you're dancing with me is for the information I have."

"Maybe. Maybe not."

"So, the next time I ask you out you will be there."

"Are you asking me out again?"

"You bet." Madelyn smiles.

Jeb laughs loudly, and the music slowly fades away. The dancers around them stop and applaud.

"Might be fun," Jeb replies. Jeb holds her hand and leads her off the dance floor.

Chapter 11

Sunset Rock

A fresh drink is sitting at Jeb's place at the table when he returns, but he doesn't want another.

Celeste laughs at both of them. "I thought about calling an Uber."

"Maybe you should have," Madelyn jokes. "You are starting to resemble a third wheel."

"It wouldn't be the same without you, Celeste," Jeb says.

"Thank you."

The tables around them are empty, and the band has taken a break. The house lights are up fully, illuminating everything in the room. The turquoise chairs and brightly patterned tablecloths look like the ones he saw in the Cabana's in Miami. Madelyn reaches across the table and touches his arm, bringing him out of his study of the décor.

"Thank you for a wonderful evening, Jeb. Now your reward," Madelyn says.

Jeb looks at her soft inviting face.

"I asked a friend of mine in the archaeology department if they had ever heard of a rock where the elders met to discuss the affairs of the tribe." She continues.

He has thought of that question as well, phrased in that way, but all of his efforts have been fruitless.

"She said that in a text from 1850, there is a reference to a sacred point." Madelyn says.

His heart nearly jumps out of his chest. This place is real.

Madelyn opens her purse and removes a faded piece of paper. "This is a copy of the text." She slides the paper across the table toward him. He picks it up slowly and reads.

The sacred rock gives wisdom to the elders. The wisdom from the sun brightens the minds of the leaders, and they pass that on to the people. We prosper because of this place. Sunset Rock.

"It is a translation, but she is sure that is the exact wording," Madelyn says.

Jeb turns the paper between his fingers, thinking. The rock now has a name, and he has seen the name before somewhere in his research. But where?

"You know where it is?" Celeste asks.

The revelation hits him like a right fist to the face. Sunset Rock overlooks the Tennessee River near the place where John Ross had his trading outpost. That rock overlooks what is now the river close to Chattanooga.

Martyn Gale had been in Chattanooga in the late 1800s. An 1887 article described his endeavor. That is why he was in Chattanooga. He was looking for Sunset Rock and what was hidden there.

"Of course, he does. Look at his face," Madelyn says.

"Maybe," Jeb says.

"You know exactly where it is, and you're taking us with you when you go looking for whatever is hidden there."

Jeb glances at Madelyn, and her eyes narrow. "Sorry, this is a one-person job," Jeb replies.

"And what happened last time you went alone," Celeste says.

"We saved you," Madelyn adds.

Maybe it will be better if he has someone there with him, just in case those guys who left him in the well make a special appearance. Jeb remains silent, thinking about the dangers that could await him either on the journey to Sunset Rock or while he is searching the area. He is certain that they could lie in many concealed places, waiting for their opportunity to strike. He doesn't want to take a header off the rock because he isn't prepared.

"We won't get in the way," Celeste says.

Jeb chuckles. "That's not what I would be worrying about."

"We can take of ourselves," Madelyn says confidently.

He is sure that they both can take care of themselves, but if he's going to meet those men again, he would rather have Clem with him. The question would be, could he convince Clem to come with him on another dangerous excursion.

"I will let you both know."

"Make it quick. Our classes start in a few days," Celeste says.

"Priorities," Jeb replies.

Jeb checks his watch, and it is almost eleven. It is later than he wanted it to be, and it is time for him to get home. Tomorrow will be an early day.

"It is time for our little party to end," Jeb says, stifling a yawn.

"One more drink?" Madelyn asks.

Jeb shakes his head. "Sorry. It is way past my bedtime."

Jeb opens his wallet and pulls out two one-hundred-dollar bills and places them on the table. "I have an early day tomorrow." He pushes his chair back and stands slowly. Madelyn and Celeste watch him with curiosity and neither one moves.

"How you getting home?" Celeste says.

Jeb smiles, and his eyes settle on Madelyn. She chews on her lip as she gazes at him. He smiles at them, taking out his phone. "I'll get a ride. Thank you both for an exciting evening."

He places the phone to his ear and walks down the steps toward the empty dance floor. Jeb knows the club will fill again very soon, and he wants to be home in his bed well before then.

As he opens the door to leave, Madelyn touches his hand. "We will take you home," she says, giving him a half smile.

Jeb nods, and they walk out of The Cabana side by side in silence.

*****

The morning comes early with the bright rays of sunlight filtering through the curtains into Jeb's bedroom. He rubs his eyes wiping the last vestiges of his sleep away. The last week, he has been busy working on his journey to Sunset Rock. Clem reluctantly agrees to accompany him only when Jeb said there isn't a possibility of danger. Jeb lied a little, but he needed his friend on this one.

Jeb reluctantly told Madelyn, but she and her friends had classes that morning that they could not miss. Jeb is relieved that they will not be there. If there is danger, he didn't want anything happening to them.

He rolls out of bed and hurriedly pulls on his shirt and cargo pants. Jeb reaches for his boots pulling them on with a huff. After he finishes getting ready, Jeb checks his pack. All his documents are there along with his flashlight and revolver. Jeb stows the revolver in his belt and heads for the door.

*****

The Saab races through town along River Street toward downtown. The airport is on the north end of Camden and requires a trip through the rush hour traffic. Jeb chews vigorously on a piece of gum, cutting the car in between two large Suburbans. He pushes the gas, accelerating away from the large Suburban assault vehicles. In a few minutes, he is through Camden and riding along the tree-lined streets that lead to the airport.

Jeb turns right into the Camden airport, stopping at the guard shack. A man in his sixties steps out from the small white box holding a clipboard.

Jeb rolls down the window. "Is Clem in?" he says, checking his watch. "I hope so. I am a little late."

The guard pushes his black hat farther up on his head. "He said Jeb Strauss would be here. Is that you?"

Jeb nods with a big smile.

"I take it you know where you're going?"

Jeb nods, and the guard opens the barrier arm. Jeb waves at the guard and drives slowly into the hangar area of the airport. Small planes roll onto the runway ready for a trip into the pale blue sky.

He parks the Saab outside a large gray hangar and opens the door. Clem ambles toward the car with his hands in his pockets and a stern look on his face.

"You're late," Clem growls.

Jeb opens his arms and smiles. "It is good to see you too old buddy."

Clem snorts opening the passenger door. "This is an easy one right. No possibility of drowning in a watery grave this time."

"None," Jeb replies.

"No CIA types shooting at us."

Jeb opens his mouth to speak but stops abruptly scratching the tip of his chin.

"No. No. I told you. No more danger," Clem says, shaking his head. He turns and walks toward the airplane hangar.

"I promise there is . . . no chance."

Clem stops and turns abruptly with his hands in his pocket. He glares at Jeb.

"Okay. Very little chance," Jeb says.

Clem throws his head backward. "There are people after you now, aren't there?" Clem scans the hangar and the other buildings at the airport. "They're out there watching us? Waiting."

Jeb holds up his hands. "Calm down. The likelihood of there being any danger is minimal."

Clem stares at him in disbelief. "You're not serious?"

"They think I'm dead. Or. At least rotting in the bottom of a deep rocky well."

"Jeez, Jeb."

Jeb chuckles. "See little chance of danger, and the reward is worth the risk."

Clem's shoulders slump, and he lowers his head walking back toward the car. "I must be insane," he says.

"I think so, yes," Jeb replies.

"All the things I do for you, Jeb. Sometimes I wonder why we're friends."

Jeb smiles. "My magnetic personality. The treasure." He holds up two fingers and then a third and fourth. "The treasure and the treasure. That covers it."

Clem shakes his head slowly and falls into the passenger's seat. Jeb slams his hand against the roof of the car and jumps into the driver's seat. He taps the steering wheel like it is a drum set, bobbing his head to the beat.

"There is definitely something wrong with you," Clem says, putting on his seatbelt.

Jeb stares at him, smiling broadly. "You keep coming back, buddy. So, I could say the same about you." Jeb laughs and starts the car. He slams the shifter into first and presses the gas. The engine revs loudly and the tires screech. A plume of smoke follows the car as it speeds away from the airplane hangar.

*****

The road up the ridge hangs precipitously on the edge of the large rocky formation. It winds up perched on blasted rock, making a firm base for the stone and asphalt. The tall sandstone outcrop towers over the roadway. If Jeb placed his arm out the window, he could almost touch the formidable rocks. The rocks blaze past the window in a blur of reds and oranges.

Jeb presses on the accelerator pushing the car faster up the inclined, curvy roadway. The valley is visible from the road, and the only thing keeping cars from plunging over the edge is a flimsy looking guardrail. He glances toward the passenger seat, and Clem's eyes are closed and he has the seat in a pale-knuckle death grip.

"You're going to kill me before we get there," Clem says.

"Never knew driving make you uncomfortable."

"Just your driving."

"Thanks."

"Don't mention it. Now, keep your eyes on the road."

Jeb presses the pedal to the floor and zips around a sharp curve squealing the tires.

"You're doing that on purpose."

Jeb laughs loudly and continues upward along the road.

After a few more minutes of excessive speed and laughs, Jeb parks in an empty gravel lot off the main road. Jeb opens the door and grabs his pack from behind the driver's seat, throwing it over his shoulder. Slamming the door behind him, Jeb looks back, and Clem is stone still.

"Any day now, buddy!" Jeb yells.

Jeb shifts his thirty-eight revolver in his belt and surveys the forest around the parking lot. There aren't any other hikers here, which is a good thing. A small trail cuts through the forest covered in a thick layer of mulch. This part of the trail should be an easy hike, but he knows that the ascent becomes more vigorous the closer to they get to the edge of the plateau.

A bird chirps overhead, welcoming them to the neighborhood. Jeb walks toward the trail with the gravel crunching under his boots. The door closes behind him, and he hears the slow shuffle of feet on gravel behind him. They start down the trail without speaking. Jeb keeps his eyes moving from one side of the path to the other. Maybe he's being a little paranoid, but he doesn't want a repeat of Stone Door. Whoever was there isn't going to take him by surprise again.

The trail curves around a giant oak tree that looks like it has been on the mountain for over a hundred years. The path dips and immediately ascends at a forty-degree angle. Large boulders from the summit litter the area around them like fallen pieces from an oversized chessboard. They move cautiously through the channel created by the tall pieces of rock, checking behind each one for unwanted visitors.

"The trail looks clear," Jeb says.

Clem looks at him with sweat pouring down his face and his chest rising and falling quickly. "How much long . . . longer?" Clem asks. He places his hands on his hips and takes a deep breath.

Jeb looks up along the steep trail. They have reached the top portion of the ridge. The sheer rock faces of sandstone loom over them. Small fissures in the rock indicate where centuries of water flowed down the mountain toward the river. The fast-flowing water creates small narrow passes through the ridge.

"Maybe fifteen, twenty minutes," Jeb replies, wiping the sweat from his face.

"Thank God."

"Sunset Rock should be right up there." Jeb points southwest. "You ready for the last leg?"

Clem nods, wiping his face with the sleeve of his shirt. Jeb walks slowly along the uneven, rocky terrain, grabbing a mushroom-shaped rock to steady himself. Through the narrow cuts and near vertical boulders, Jeb emerges onto a solid stone slab marked with small indentions. The outcrop is the size of a tennis court but without the smoothness.

Jeb turns and looks off the perch into the green valley below. The river meanders between the hills and ridges from downtown westward. It stretches out endlessly until the sparkling reflection from the water is lost behind a tall ridge.

"Let's get to work," Jeb says, looking down at the light-orange stone.

"What am I looking for?"

Jeb huffs. "A marker. A glyph. Words not in English."

"I suppose this Steve hearts Valerie isn't it."

"Don't think John Ross hid a clue in that."

Jeb leans close to the stone slab running his fingers along the coarse grains. He feels the sand grains move against his skin like sandpaper. He methodically searches from the center to the edge, looking intently at every part of the exposed rock. The minutes tick by slowly and each one is as fruitless as the one before.

What if the steady rainfall has removed the symbol? If that is the case, the hunt for the treasure ends here on this large slab of stone. Backward and forward, he continues scouring the sandy surface. The tips of his fingers are raw from brushing against the grains of sand, and his eyes ache from straining to see something that could be hidden. After another two passes along the rock, Jeb stands and walks to the edge of the large rock. The river below looks calm and still like a landscape painting.

Jeb sits at the edge of Sunset Rock with his feet dangling off the ledge. Is this the rock of the elders? Is this where they found enlightenment for the direction of their people? An endless number of questions pour into his mind as he stares at the sea of green in the valley below. The birds chirp loudly as if they are laughing at his failure.

"Looks like it's not here," Clem says, breathing heavily beside him.

"From the information I received, this is the place," Jeb replies without taking his eyes off the valley.

"I don't know what to tell you, buddy. You've been on your hands and knees for the last hour looking for something that isn't here."

"The Sun Makes Fire That Shines Into The Valley. From This Rock Our Fathers Have Watched Our People Grow Into A Powerful Nation And From This Rock, It Will Reveal The Fortunes of Our People," Jeb recites. The words from Stone Door are inscribed in his mind.

"Not sure what all that means, but there ain't no fire, door, or treasure here. Can't even see the sun through the clouds," Clem says, tapping the rock with his fist. "Solid. Nothing here."

Clem is right, and that stings. Nothing is perched on the mountaintop indicating that this is a sacred place to anyone except people etching their initials in the hard rock pronouncing their unending love. Jeb takes a deep breath, tossing a small pebble into the valley below. Sometimes as a treasure hunter, Jeb fails. Sometimes even after he has conducted a hundred hours of research, the treasure isn't there.

Chapter 12

In the Fire

Jeb picks up another stone and heaves it out into the emptiness of sky above the valley.

"Time to go, Jeb." Clem says.

Jeb looks up at the thick clouds drifting across the sky. Small beams of light break through the puffy white barrier, creating small rings of gold. This spot is definitely a beautiful overlook. The sky is vast and endless. Pair that with the view of the valley and the river, and this is a great spot to view creation.

Jeb stands slowly and turns away for the edge of the giant slab of rock. Small beams of sunlight strike the surface of the sandstone. The quartz crystals sparkle in the vibrant rays, creating a dazzling light show. His heart beats faster, and he steps back, glancing from sparkling area to sparkling area.

"What are you doing?" Clem asks.

"Shhhhhhh!"

Finally, the sun emerges fully from the cloud cover, and the rock below shimmers radiantly like a strobe light. Jeb takes the phone from his pocket and snaps a few pictures. "Oh my." He says, looking at the images on the screen.

"What did you find?" Clem asks excitedly.

The despair Jeb felt a few minutes ago has subsided, and the excitement of finding something that others have not flows freely through him. "It's a symbol," Jeb says, enlarging the picture. "See this."

Clem stands beside him, peering at the bright image on the screen. "I don't see anything other than flashes of light."

"Those flashes of light create a picture. See." Jeb points.

"I still don't see nothing," Clem replies. "I think you're seeing what you want to see."

If he had brought his drone, he could have taken an aerial picture. That would have allowed him to see the whole clue. Maybe there was more than one image. Jeb moves to the other side of the rock and snaps pictures. He wants a photographic record of the entire slab so he can study it later.

He looks at each photograph, studying the lights and the lines that connect the sparkles of light.

"Wow," he says. "There is more than one. Look, this first one is a V with horizontal lines connecting both sides of the letter. Wonder what that means?"

"Ah, Jeb," Clem calls.

"Not sure about this one."

"Jeb."

Jeb raises his head, and Clem glares at him with his arms held high in the air. Behind Clem, two men with shoulder-length jet black hair stand, pointing the barrel of a pistol at them.

"You know firearms are against the law on park grounds," Jeb says, placing the phone in his pocket.

The one on the right with the chiseled face grins. "We will take our chances."

Instantly, Jeb recognizes the voice as the guy from Stone Door. This is the guy that cut the rope ladder and left him there.

"I'm not sure how you made it out of your tomb, Mr. Strauss, but this time you will not be so lucky."

Jeb feels the cold from his thirty-eight against his skin, but he isn't that fast. Before he reached his belt, they would fill him with plenty of holes. Jeb backs away from them toward the edge of the large rock. He stops abruptly with his heels on the very edge of the cliff.

"Don't you guys something better to do than hassle hikers trying to enjoy some of Tennessee's scenic beauty," Jeb says.

"You are more than a hiker, Mr. Strauss."

"Look, guys, me and my friend here are just out experiencing nature that's it. So, whatever this is," Jeb says, pointing toward their guns, "I think we can work something out."

Clem is a still as one of the boulders along the trail up to Sunset Rock. Jeb tries to get his attention.

"You know this is a particularly crowded overlook," Jeb says, motioning for Clem to join him at the edge. If he can keep them talking, maybe they can escape somehow.

The tall slender man steps to the right and looks back toward the trail. The barrel of his pistol is still pointing at Clem. The other man glares at Jeb with a strange sneer. "I don't think things can be worked out. You see. You have barreled headlong into something that you truly do not understand," Square Jaw says.

Clem's eyes are wide as he turns to Jeb motioning him toward him. Clem faces the two assailants with his arms high in the air. He slowly backs toward Jeb at the edge of the ridge. Square Jaw moves closer to them, and the sneer never leaves his face.

"We are up here looking at the rock formations, and that is it," Jeb protests.

Square Jaw's eyes narrow. "It is convenient that you have visited the hidden river, the well at Stone Door, and the Rock of Fire. It must be a fantastic coincidence to have someone explore all three places in succession if they are merely hikers exploring the natural world, as you say."

Clem stops beside him. "Why do I agree to go with you? You said there was no chance this would happen," Clem whispers.

Jeb shakes his head without taking his eyes off Square Jaw and his friend.

"You got me." Jeb laughs. "What can I say? Obviously, you know what I'm after. You could save me some time and tell me exactly where it is."

The man stops yards in front of them, pointing the gun at Jeb then at Clem.

"Be a pal, friend," Jeb continues. "Tell us where it is."

"You will never find what you seek," Square Jaw spits.

"Ah. That is where you're wrong, Geronimo."

Jeb watches Square Jaw's face tense, and he grits his teeth.

"You're going to get us killed." Clem whispers."

Jeb smiles. He is going to get out of this. He isn't dying on this slab of cold rock. He glances over his shoulder at the emptiness behind him. The rock they are perched on is forty or fifty feet above the sloping side of the ridge. But. a few tall white oak trees grow upward from the slope toward the overlook. That's it!

"Oh no," Clem shakily whispers.

Jeb nods his head slowly, looking at the two men standing in front of them.

The slender man rushes forward from the edge of the trail waving his gun around. "You will pay for your insults."

"Get ready to jump," Jeb whispers to Clem.

"You've lost your mind."

"Just get ready. Jump toward the branches of the oak tree."

"What?"

"You will see it."

Jeb smiles at the two men, but Square Jaw lowers his pistol, glaring at him. "The treasure of the elders will remain hidden. Our brotherhood has protected its location for almost two hundred years. We have killed many who have started on the path to our ancestral riches."

"Ready?" Jeb whispers.

"You are just another greedy treasure seeker who will get his reward. Your people stole everything from us, but not this time." He raises the gun. His eyes are black, cold, and detached.

"Now," Jeb says. Instantly, Jeb leaps from the rock. The air roars through his ears as he falls with his arms flailing. The small pops of the nine-millimeter cut through the rushing air around him. Jeb strikes a large branch on the tall oak tree, causing him to spin in the air. He grabs at the bark, but it slips through his fingers, and he falls farther, colliding with the hard thick branches.

Clem screams above him, but Jeb can't see where. Jeb bounces from branch to branch like a ball in a pinball machine. Finally, he grabs onto a branch the size of his leg securely. His head aches, and he feels the warm trickle of blood flowing from his brow. Scratches on his arms weep blood droplets.

He looks up, and Clem is bear-hugging the trunk of the large oak muttering softly. Jeb cranes his neck, and Square Jaw and his accomplice stand at the rock face. They pull the trigger, and fire erupts from the barrels.

"Get down here, Clem!" Jeb yells. The bullets strike the trunk above his head, and he rotates to the other side of the tree.

Clem shuffles down toward him, shielded from the fire by the large tree. The bullets whizz through the leaves and *thunk* against the branches. Jeb looks at the ground eight feet below. *Thunk. Thunk.* He raises his head, and Clem is almost on top of him. Jeb pushes off from the tree and falls to the sloping ground below.

Jeb hits the uneven ground and rolls a few yards down the slope. His body slams into a large boulder, sending shockwaves of pain through his shoulder.

"AGH!" Jeb yells. He rolls onto his knees and looks toward Sunset Rock. He can't see the two men who were firing at them. "Clem. AGH," Jeb says, getting to his feet. "Let's go. We are going to have company."

Clem stumbles away from the tree toward him. "I can't believe you've done it to me again, Jeb. This is it. Last time."

Jeb's shoulder aches as he steps around the boulder with Clem following him. Blood falls onto his shirt mixed with the sweat from his face, creating splotches on the fabric.

"I think we can make it back to the car before they get there," Jeb says, breathing heavily.

They hurry between the tall boulders, following a deer trail that cuts through the dense foliage surrounding the giant rocks. Jeb wipes the sweat from his brow, thinking about how they found him. He has been very careful, and no one had trailed them on their way up the mountain. It doesn't make sense. Something doesn't add up.

"I don't think we should go back to the car," Clem says.

"We're a long way from home," Jeb replies.

"I would rather walk than run into those guys again."

"If we hurry, we won't have to worry about it."

The trail ahead descends steeply down a leaf-strewn path between tall oaks. Jeb rushes forward, forgetting the small throb of pain emanating from his side and shoulder. He touches the thirty-eight snugly lodged in his belt. This time he will be ready if they make a reappearance.

The trees grow sparse, and the fading sunlight cast small golden spheres on the forest floor. The gravel parking lot is directly ahead of them, and Jeb pulls his revolver from the holster. He eases it into his front pocket with this finger on the trigger guard.

"Keep your eyes open," Jeb says. He turns, and Clem is leaning over with his hands on his knees. He looks up his face bright red with exertion.

Jeb looks away from Clem and searches the surroundings around the parking lot. His Saab is the only car in the lot. Do they know where he parked? He is certain that they do, but where is their car? The area around the parking lot is clear. Jeb can't see any movement or shadow. He tightens the grip on his revolver and creeps slowly from behind a tall tree with Clem trailing on his heels.

He picks up speed, meandering around a crape myrtle that stands at the edge of the gravel lot. His heart pounds in his chest, and he takes one last look around the parking lot. Taking a deep breath, Jeb burst from the cover of the trees and races across the gravel parking lot. The gravel crunches under his hurried steps as he nears the car. Jeb rests his back against the door and fumbles in his pocket for his key.

"Hurry up," Clem growls, kneeling beside him.

Finally, Jeb's fingers grasp the key, and he pulls it out quickly. With a small click, the lock disengages from the door. Jeb opens it and crawls into the driver's seat, keeping his head below the wheel.

Clem climbs into the backseat and lays across the floorboard. "Let's get out of here Jeb," Clem says.

Jeb rams the key into the ignition and starts the car. The car comes to life. He closes the door and looks over the steering wheel.

"Oh great." Jeb exhales.

The two men race down the trail toward them. Jeb slams the Saab into gear and rams his foot onto the gas pedal. Gravel and smoke billow out behind the car as it slides sideways on the loose gravel. Jeb turns the wheel sharply, trying to correct the spin. The car jerks in the other direction. He sees the men pointing their guns at him and fire erupting from the barrel.

"Please don't hit my car," Jeb says.

"Get us out of here, Jeb!" Clem cries.

"I'm working on it."

The car fishtails again drifting from side to side in short swift jerks. The tires glide across the loose gravel, trying to get a firm grip. Jeb slams his foot on the gas, and the car lurches forward onto the asphalt. The tires bark, and they speed away from their pursuers. Jeb looks in the rearview mirror at the two men shouting. An SUV pulls up beside them, and the men jump inside. The SUV chases the Saab.

Chapter 13

Another Escape

The Saab hugs the sharp turns on the two-lane mountain road. The trees blaze by the windows in a green and brown blur.

"Don't be alarmed or anything, Clem, but they're chasing us," Jeb says, his eyes darting from the rearview mirror to the road in front of them.

"You've really done it this time," Clem grumbles from the back floorboard.

"Why are you cowering on the floor?"

"When they start shooting, this will be the safest place."

"They won't get that close." Jeb laughs.

"You're crazy. You know that?"

Jeb laughs loudly and accelerates around a sharp curve. The tires squeal, trying to grip the smooth roadway. "WOOOHOOOOO," Jeb screams, turning the wheel to the right.

"I'm going to be sick," Clem says.

"No puking in the car."

The Saab races farther ahead of the trailing SUV. Jeb sees the two men's arms out the window, firing their guns at his car. He speeds faster down the mountain, crossing the double yellow line to catch the turn without braking. The SUV falls farther and farther behind them, but Jeb keeps his foot on the gas.

He steers the car around another sharp corner, crossing the double yellow line again. Drifting into the outside lane without losing speed, he breathes a sigh of relief. They should be home free now. That SUV can't keep up with his sports car. A smile stretches across Jeb's face, but he keeps his foot on the pedal.

"I think we're okay," Jeb says. "You can peel yourself off the floor."

"UGGGHHH."

The road straightens ahead of them, and another car is coming up the mountain. Jeb glances in the mirror, but he doesn't see the trailing SUV. As his eyes return to the roadway, the car coming toward them veers into their lane.

"Not good. Not good," Jeb says.

"What now?" Clem groans.

"A bit more excitement, is all. Hold on."

Jeb swerves into a slow car pull off lane, narrowly missing the front bumper of a dark sedan. The rear of the car swings to the right skidding on the gravel.

"Come on, grip," Jeb says. The guardrail inches closer to them, and the long drop to the valley below. "I never realized how great the view was from up here."

The back tires of the Saab grip the road, and the car shoots from the gravel into the main roadway. Jeb slams his foot on the accelerator and steers the car around another sharp corner. The tires squeal loudly, letting him know that seventy miles an hour on a mountain road is all that they can handle. Jeb glances in the mirror, and the sedan barrels around the corner after them.

"This is getting fun." Jeb says.

"They're still back there?"

"Yep, more than one."

"Don't tell me how many."

The roadway descends rapidly as they near the bottom of the ridge. Jeb's eyes dart from the straight road ahead to the speeding dark car behind him. He should be able to outrun them, but they know who he is and probably where he lives. He can't go back home, that is certain.

Jeb drums his fingers on the steering wheel with his eyes darting from the mirror to the road. *Where are we going to go?*

"Oh man," Jeb says. The black sedan speeds toward him. "Their car is modified."

The Saab groans loudly with Jeb pushing the pedal to the floor. The small sports car jerks and speeds down the sloping road toward the Highway 36 intersection.

A smaller road feeds into the road Jeb is on a few hundred yards before Highway 36. A large SUV races along it.

"Come on! Come on!" Jeb screams.

"Dare I ask?" Clem says from his prone position on the floor.

"No time." Jeb looks from the approaching SUV to the speeding sedan behind him. "This is going to be close." The Saab flies by the intersections just as the SUV careens into the roadway. Jeb swerves to the right, missing the bumper of the SUV by inches. His heart pounds, and his fingers shake.

He hears a loud *bang* from behind him. The SUV and the sedan spin in a heap of folded metal kicking dust and clouds of smoke into the air. Jeb races away from the crash scene.

"I think we are going to be all right," he says, exhaling loudly.

"Take me home," Clem says.

"I was thinking . . ."

"No! Home."

Jeb slows at Highway 36 but doesn't stop. He accelerates onto the main highway, keeping his eyes on the rearview mirror. Relief courses through his body, but the question of what he is going to do still fills his mind. He will drop Clem off at the airport and then figure out what he is going to do next.

He has the pictures of the fire pattern on Sunset Rock. The only thing that is needed is time to figure out where the clue leads. Unfortunately, he will need another place to research and decide on a plan of action.

CHAPTER 14

IN HIDING

The moon shines brightly above, showering the front yard of a two-story Victorian home in a pale golden glow. English ivy grows along a trellis from the bottom of the house to the second-floor patio.

The Saab sits on the road in front of the four-columned home. Jeb looks behind him and in front. After he dropped Clem off at the airport, he had decided on where to go. He opens the door and grabs his pack. He walks along the cobblestone sidewalk toward the large oak front door.

Standing on the front porch, he lightly raps on the door. He searches the shadows for any movement. The dark green shrubs sway slightly on the currents of a soft breeze. The porch is illuminated with a fabricated light that pales in comparison to the natural glow from the moon.

After a second, the door slowly opens. "What are you doing here?" Madelyn asks.

Jeb smiles broadly, "I needed a bit more of your expertise."

"Of Course you do." Madelyn says, motioning him to come inside. He stands in the foyer, looking up at an exquisite polished black and gold chandelier. The vibrant light bathes the mahogany floors in its brilliance. The house looks like it never left the Gilded Age.

Madelyn closes the door and walks through the foyer into the spacious living room. "Are you coming?" she asks.

"Sorry. This place is like a museum," Jeb says.

The living room has wood-paneled walls, polished to a mirrored shine. A white couch and settee sit in the center of the room on a vast oriental rug.

"This is my parents' house. They allow me to use it while I'm in school. But I do like the art deco style," Madelyn says, motioning toward the smooth white marble fireplace.

Madelyn sits on the plush white sofa and places her feet on the oversized wooden coffee table. "Take a seat," she says.

Jeb drops his bag on the floor and gazes up at the bronze light fixtures.

"You never said why you're paying me a visit so late."

"I did." He smiles. "I found some information about the John Ross treasure, and I was hoping you could help me out."

Madelyn laughs. "So, my friend's information was right?"

Jeb nods his head slowly. "They actually chiseled the rock away from the large quartz crystals, so when the sun hit it, Sunset Rock blazed like a fire. It was a marvelous sight to behold."

"Not sure how much I can help you. It is my friend that you want."

"I think you know more than you let on."

Madelyn's bright green eyes sparkle, and she studies him intently. A small delicate smile forms on her face. She pushes a strand of brown hair behind her ear. "Maybe."

The clock on the mantle chimes loudly with ten consecutive dings. Even though it is late for a twenty-four-year-old treasure hunter who has been up since daybreak, he isn't tired at all. After all the running and escaping, he is wide awake.

Jeb opens his bag and removes his journal. He thumbs through the pages and stops at a page with a bent corner. The clue from Stone Door is written at the top of the page.

"The Sun Makes Fire That Shines Into The Valley. From This Rock Our Fathers Have Watched Our People Grow Into A Powerful Nation And From This Rock, It Will Reveal The Fortunes of Our People."

He glances from the page to Madelyn reclining on the couch. She looks at the page with a slight smile creasing the corner of her mouth.

"What will you write below those words?" she says.

Jeb grabs his phone and opens the pictures of the glittering lights on the solid stone slab.

"I didn't find any words written on the rock, but look at the pattern of the quartz crystals," Jeb replies. Jeb pushes the book to her side of the table and moves to the seat beside her on the couch. "Look at this," he says, holding the screen for Madelyn to see.

Madelyn narrows her eyes and studies the perfectly clear image on the screen. He traces a line between the lights. "See this first one looks like a V with continual horizontal lines moving from one side to the other." She nods slowly. "And this one looks like three continuous Ms with an X below it."

She takes the phone from his hand and draws it close to her, tilting the screen right then left.

Jeb picks up the journal from the table and delicately draws the pattern of the lights from the screen. After putting the final touches on the drawing, he looks up at Madelyn.

"I have an idea of what those mean. They weren't in the syllabary that a friend of mine gave me, but there are similar features to some of the words. But it is just a guess."

"Since I've known you, Jeb Strauss, I would bet that you never guess when it comes to finding the truth." Madelyn smiles, laying the phone on the table.

She is right. He is almost always sure of the location or the answer to any question before moving onward. This time he wants a second opinion, and he wants that opinion from the person who provided valuable information in locating Sunset Rock. Jeb is absolutely positive that Madelyn is the source and not a friend like she has led him to believe.

"You're right. I'm looking for the truth, and I need your help in finding it."

"Not sure I'm the best source. I'm an economics nerd. Remember?"

"An economics nerd who pointed me to Sunset Rock."

Her eyes narrow, and the edge of her lower lip curls upward. "That was from a friend of mine," she says, brushing a few stray hairs from her face.

"It was you," Jeb says, looking at her shrewdly.

"Have you been checking up on me, Jeb Strauss?"

"Like you said, I like to know what I am getting into. I like to know the truth."

"Hopefully, your investigation was fun."

Jeb looks from her delicate face and dancing emerald eyes to his book.

"Spending all that time on researching me. Like I'm one of the treasures that you desperately seek. It is a bit flattering."

That is a bit extreme, he thinks as he looks at his drawings, but he does find her captivating. Well-educated on many different topics and interested in the intricacies of his profession.

"You make me sound like a stalker." Jeb laughs.

She moves closer to him, and her arm brushes against his. "Let's see what we can do," Madelyn says slowly. Her hot breath flows across the space between his neck and shoulder.

Jeb sets the book between them. "I think this," he says, pointing to the three continuous figures with the X below it, "represents a mountain and the treasure under it."

"That makes sense," she says.

"The V with the horizontal lines, I'm not sure about that one."

He glances from the book to her face. Madelyn looks intently at the book, slowly tracing the pictures with her index finger. She appears lost in thought and doesn't notice that her brown hair has fallen across her face. Jeb fights the urge to return the wayward strands behind her ear. Her eyes dart from the page and meet his.

"If the treasure is in a mountain," she says slowly without taking her eyes off his, "there has to be an entrance." She chews on her lip after she speaks. Her bright green eyes shine like beacons.

Jeb looks away and stands. He paces from his seat on the couch to the marble fireplace. He needs to keep his mind clear, and sitting on the couch that close to her makes his mind hazy. He strides back toward the seat without looking at her. Slowly, his mind moves away from the sight of her hypnotic eyes to the words she has spoken.

"The V could be an entrance. A cave entrance, but what do the horizontal lines mean?"

After a few minutes of pacing from the couch to the fireplace, Madelyn's voice brings him out of his trance. "Do you always do this?" she asks.

He smiles. "Sometimes."

He places his hand on the cold marble mantle and adjusts his dark-rimmed glasses. "What mountain did John Ross use?" When looking at the footprint of the Cherokee Nation, there were numerous mountains, and many of them have vast caverns under them. That leaves too many places for them to explore personally. What else are those quartz crystal patterns on Sunset Rock trying to tell him? There has to be something else there.

"I think the possibility of him using a cave system that was close to home is very likely," Madelyn says.

Jeb nods. He had thought of that. John Ross returned to Chattanooga after leaving Oklahoma. That gives credence to his belief that it has to be somewhere around this small southern city.

"And it looks like the . . . Can I see they picture again?" Madelyn asks.

Jeb pushes away from the mantle and opens his phone. The bright light from the screen flashes across his glasses. He looks at the picture of the shining lights on the slab of rock. The distinctive three peaks of the mountains with the X below. He sits down beside her and holds the screen so that she can see it.

The three peaks indicate the exact location. It isn't simply indicating the treasure lies under a nameless mountain, but it is the exact mountain. Look at the where the lines of the cross are," Jeb says excitedly. The cross is found under the mountain on the left. "The three peaks. I would bet they are—" Madelyn starts.

"Elder, Raccoon, and Aetna Mountain," they say at the same time.

Jeb looks at her, and her bright green eyes dance. "The X is below the western mountain." Madelyn says.

"Aetna Mountain," Jeb says, smiling.

"Wow," Madelyn says. "That is something."

Jeb has read plenty about the Cherokee since he began searching for the John Ross treasure. Aetna Mountain was part of the Cherokee Nation until they were forcibly removed in 1838, and it protected the home of a Cherokee warrior named Dragging Canoe.

"Hiding the treasure there would be significant," Madelyn continues.

"Yes, it would. John Ross paying homage to the warrior that established the settlement near Chattanooga," Jeb says. "Hiding your treasure there is quite symbolic."

Jeb takes his book and writes feverishly on the page.

With a final flourish, he stows his pen in the spine of the journal. His hand jumps as Madelyn's hand slowly moves along his forearm.

"I guess you will be leaving now," she says with her eyes wide. "Since I helped you locate the John Ross treasure."

A voice in his mind screams out loud. *You should let her come along. She has been invaluable in finding the resting place of the treasure.* But a part of him doesn't want to expose her to the dangers that go along with the search. He doesn't want anything to happen to her.

Jeb stands slowly placing the journal in his pocket. He looks down at her round delicate face. "I'm sorry. I would love to take you along."

"But it could be dangerous, and you don't want me getting hurt," Madelyn finishes.

"Something like that."

"You don't think I can handle myself."

"I didn't say that."

"A woman couldn't possibly succeed in the adventure business. Right?"

Jeb walks toward the door. He knows that she would have no problem with the hiking or the caving part of the hunt. Madelyn is athletic and strong. She is smart and very adept at seeing the connection between clues and where they lead. Madelyn would be an asset, and with her fast thinking and analysis, her expertise would be irreplaceable.

Jeb grabs the door handle and closes his eyes.

"So that's it," Madelyn says. Jeb turns slowly, and she is still sitting on the couch with her feet on the coffee table. "You're going to leave me behind after I helped you solve the last part of the riddle. You came to me because you knew what I have to offer. You trust me, and there might be other clues. You need me, Jeb Strauss."

He shakes his head slowly. That is going a bit too far. She has been a good source of information, but he doesn't need her. He gets the feeling that she is talking about more than finding treasure, and he doesn't want to venture into something like that. Jeb remains frozen with his hand gripping the door.

"I can help you, and you know it."

Madelyn jumps to her feet and walks away from the couch. "Let me get my gear," she says cheerily.

She leaves the room, and Jeb looks at his watch. That didn't go the way he had planned, but it might be a benefit having her along. Like she said, she would be able to help if there were other clues hidden inside the cavern.

Five minutes later, she returns to the living room carrying a duffel bag and wearing a pair of navy-blue cargo pants and a tight white T-shirt. She has her shoulder-length brown hair pulled tightly into a braid.

Jeb smiles. *Crawling through mud and scraping against rocks will be much better with Madelyn than Clem*, he thinks as he opens the door. At least, he won't have to hear Clem's complaints about the chance of death again and again.

He steps through the door and waits on the porch. Madelyn closes the door and stands beside him.

"I brought this too," she says, lifting her shirt and displaying the handle of a forty-five. "Always be prepared, is what my father always says." Madelyn laughs as she steps in front of him and descends the stairs.

She is full of surprises, Jeb thinks as he follows her down the cobblestone sidewalk toward the car. She opens the door and throws her bag on the seat. She looks at him with a broad smile.

"Let's have some fun," she says, hopping into the car.

Jeb climbs into the driver's seat looking up the street and down the street. The men that came after Clem and

Jeb on the mountain are still out there. He closes the door and starts the engine and quickly shifts the car into gear. Madelyn touches his hand before he can take it off the gear shifter.

"Don't worry." She says.

Looking at her soft features in the pale glow of the dome light sends a shiver up his spine. A nervous he has never felt before settles over him. He gives her a pained smile pushing the thoughts of danger away. He will keep her safe. That is a promise.

CHAPTER 15

RUINS

The drive from Sewanee to the sixteen-hundred-foot ridge along the Tennessee River takes a little longer than Jeb had expected, but they arrive at the point of the ridge that overlooks the river at one thirty. The full moon illuminates the tall oak and pine trees that move from the small tar-and-chip roadway as far as he can see.

Jeb opens his phone and pulls up the topo map of Aetna Mountain. It almost looks like a flat tabletop with small crevices cut through the rock by centuries of running water. Where they are parked is desolate and quiet. The last sign of life they passed was in the town of Whiteside.

"Well, here we are. If our projections are right, our cave entrance should be out on this point," he says, glancing up at her from the glowing screen.

"It is crazy how this part of the ridge," she points to the part of Aetna Mountain that protrudes toward the river, "combined with all the others looks exactly like the shining quartz crystals from Sunset Rock."

Madelyn is right. It is like whoever carved the rock around those crystals was creating an aerial view of Aetna and the surrounding peaks. The Cherokee people were truly ingenious. They were far more advanced than history gives them credit for.

Jeb lowers the window and turns the engine off. The cicadas and tree frogs sing loudly in the night, and he leans back in his seat. "We will get started first thing in the morning," Jeb says, closing his eyes.

"You don't want to get started now?" Madelyn asks.

"It's dark."

"What kind of adventurer are you?" She punches his shoulder. "Look out there. You can see all the way to the river in this moonlight."

Jeb opens his eyes and stares at her. "You're not going to let me sleep, are you?"

"Not when we are this close."

Madelyn's pushes the door open and steps out into the warm summer night. The sky is cloudless, and the dazzling stars shine brightly from the dark curtain of space. Jeb yawns loudly, letting her know that it is the middle of the night, but she acts like she doesn't hear him.

"Tick tock," she says, her head popping into the open window.

"All right." Jeb sighs.

This cheeriness at two in the morning is much different from the usual conditions of his quests. With Clem, there is always grumbling and complaining. Jeb misses his friend a little as he opens the door and rolls out of the car. He slings his pack over his shoulder.

"I think we go this way." Madelyn points toward the M-shaped point on the map.

The trees are thick, and the leaf canopy is lush and green. The gray bark of the oaks is visible in the light.

"Going to be a slow go," Jeb says, closing the door and approaching the rear of the car. He opens the trunk and removes the duffle bag. He looks around the dark and lonely road, searching for anything that doesn't belong. It might be paranoia, but he prefers to be prepared.

The cicadas chirp louder, and the frogs raise their voices to match. Madelyn strides away from the road toward the tall line of oak trees that are twenty feet from the roadway. Jeb takes the flashlight from his pack and follows her.

They step into the cover of the tall trees, and the light from the moon is almost extinguished with only small splotches of blue light falling on the leafy ground. Jeb flips on his light, and a bright yellow beam brightens the darkness. There isn't a trail to follow, only gaps between the large trunks of the trees.

The sounds of the forest are alive at this early hour, and the creatures serenade the visitors on their walk. After thirty minutes of meandering through the thickets and undergrowth, they emerge into an open area where they can see the dark purple sky. Jeb checks his map. "I think we are . . ."

"Oh my," Madelyn says.

Jeb looks up from the map and looks at her. She is near the edge of the clearing, kneeling beside something that he can't make out. He walks over, shining his bright tactical flashlight near her feet.

"Look at this."

Jeb shines the light on the circular stone structure that is two feet tall. Dead grass and leaves cover the base.

"You know what this is?" She exclaims.

He hurries a few yards into the shelter of the trees to the west. He shines his light excitedly. The beam falls on another small stone structure the same size as the first. His heart beats wildly in his chest.

"Cairns," Jeb says.

"Yep. Used by the Cherokee to indicate locations of importance."

Jeb licks his lips. He is happy that she talked him into searching now instead of the morning. They could find the treasure and be back to the car before sunrise. "See if you can find another one. They should be in a pattern pointing the way."

"They will point the way to the entrance. The V with the horizontal lines," Madelyn says.

Jeb takes his journal and flips through the pages quickly. He stops at a blank page and moves his pencil across the surface drawing the locations of the two cairns. "Where . . ."

"Over here, Jeb," Madelyn says.

Madelyn stands fifteen yards ahead of Jeb beneath the sagging branches of a young oak tree. "Number three," she says, touching the stacked stones with her hands. "How many do you think there are?"

Jeb glances from the page to the next structure. They are in a linear pattern like an arrow. He looks to the right. There should be another sequence of rock structures in that direction. If he can find them, he should be able to find where the two lines of cairns meet.

He looks at the map and the drawing. They are pointing in the direction of the setting sun. The cave entrance will possibly correspond to that.

Jeb walks through the thicket and emerges onto a small trail. The leaves have been trampled onto the pathway by animals over the years leaving a well-defined trail through the towering trees. He turns left, walking along the narrow passage past the white pine and oak.

"Jeb?" Madelyn calls from the other side of the thicket. "Where are you?"

"I'm looking for the other side of the V," he says. "Keep following the cairns. We should meet at the entrance to the shaft."

An owl hoots overhead letting them know that it sees them. The sound is eerie and chilling, and considering he is hunting for Cherokee treasure, an owl hooting sometimes is considered a bad omen.

He follows the trail slowly rotating the light from one side to the other. The light flashes across a pile of rocks on the right side of the path. He hurries forward, searching the thicket for others, and another one appears on the same trajectory. After another ten minutes, the trees thin and the leaf-strewn trail becomes rocky.

"Glad you finally made it," Madelyn says, sitting on a flat piece of sandstone. Jeb walks over to her, and down below them the moonlight glitters across the surface of the river.

"This is where they meet," Jeb says, looking down at the valley. "I didn't see a vertical shaft or anything." He shines the light on the ground, moving around in circles, but the slabs of sandstone are whole without any crevices or caves.

Jeb looks at the rock she is sitting on and shakes his head. "That is the last cairn," he says. Jeb rushes to the pile of rocks and searches all around, but there isn't an opening. Where could it be? He sits beside her, searching the ridges extending out toward the northwest. "Surely not."

"What?" she asks.

Jeb lays flat on the cold stone and glances over the edge of the cliff. The rock wall is fifty feet tall, and it reflects the light from the moon except for one small circular opening that remains black. The shadow is halfway down the face of the cliff. Jeb stands quickly, pulling his pack off his shoulders.

"It's down there," he says.

Jeb stows the book in his pocket and quickly opens the bag. He pulls out a series of ropes and clips.

"And were going after it?" Madelyn says.

"Yep," Jeb replies. "You ever rappelled?"

"What do you think?"

Being a student at the University of the South, Jeb bets that she does this every weekend. He ties the ropes securely to the large slab and sandstone and drops them over the edge. They both dangle near the circular opening in the cliff below.

Jeb tosses her a harness, and she looks at him with a smirk.

"You not helping me put this on?" she asks.

Jeb puts on his harness and buckles it around his waist. "You've done this before. You don't need me getting in your way," Jeb replies.

Madelyn laughs and slowly dons the harness. Jeb grabs the ropes and waits. She buckles the front and slowly walks toward him.

"Ready," she says.

They secure the ropes to their harnesses in silence. The owl hoots loudly from a nearby tree. Its bright eyes shine from the top branches of a tall oak tree.

If this is a bad omen, let's get it over with. Jeb drops over the side of the rock face, holding the rope tightly in his hands.

He slowly walks down the smooth sandstone cliff holding onto the rope. Madelyn scampers down the rope like a professional, jumping ten feet at a time and landing against the rock face. Madelyn quickly makes it to the opening and disappears inside. Jeb hurries down the length of rope and hooks his feet onto the edge of the opening. He pulls himself into the darkness of the cave.

"Madelyn?" he says, unlatching the harness and tossing it on the cave floor. She doesn't answer. He strains his ears for any sound, but there's nothing.

"Madelyn?"

Switching on the flashlight, the darkness subsides in a sea of bright yellow light. The opening is the size of a small foyer with a ceiling that is at least seven feet high. Two pathways lead away from the chamber, one on the left the other on the right. Jeb crosses the rocky flow to the passage on the right.

"Madelyn!" His voice echoes through the tunnel.

He waits, but she still doesn't respond. "Great," he says, removing the thirty-eight from his belt. Jeb starts down the passage on the right, stepping carefully on the uneven rock. He strains his ears, listening for any sound. Small drops of water against stone sound like explosions in the quietness of the cavern.

"Where are you?" he asks. He waits for a few seconds.

He never should have allowed her to join him. Every adventure that he has gone on, there has been a near-death experience. If something happens to her, he will be responsible. How will he live with himself if she is hurt? The feeling flows over him.

The passageway descends deeper into the mountain, the air growing cooler with each passing step. The light from the flashlight shines on the wall, and visible in the glow are small characters and images. He is on the right track.

"Madelyn?"

He strains his ears listening for a reply, but she doesn't respond. A faint tapping sound drifts through the cool cave air. He holds his breath listening for a pattern to the sound of the *tinks.* His mouth is dry as he waits. She could have fallen into a deep hole and tapping the rocks could be the only way she can communicate.

Tink. Tink. Tink

He starts moving forward again into the depths of the cavern, carefully searching along the floor and walls for an opening. *Tink. Tink. Tink.* The sounds grow louder with each step forward.

"Madelyn? Is that you?"

The passage makes a sharp turn to the right. *Tink.* Jeb stops and peers around the corner shining the light along the floor and walls. The floor is wet from the dripping water overhead, and the walls are made of solid limestone. This place resembles a tomb. *Tink. Tink.*

Jeb walks slowly along the wet stone, being careful not to slip on the smooth surface. The light shines brightly on the cold gray stone that encases the tunnel. A few yards farther, the passage opens into a large amphitheater-like formation. The ceiling is twenty feet above, and stalactites grow downward toward the base of the cavern.

The stalagmites growing from the floor are thick and resemble the stumps of a cut forest. Jeb moves around the obstacles carefully looking for depressions or caves that venture deeper into the mountain.

Tink. Tink. The sound grows louder, and as Jeb steps around a giant pillar of rock, he stares at drawings and words etched on the smooth stone walls. Some of the pictures are six to seven feet tall, and the writing is intensive like it is a giant page of a book.

CHAPTER 16

NOTES FROM THE PAST

Jeb approaches the wall and stares up at the writing. He scans the words rapidly. When he reaches the bottom, his eyes catch the reflection from his flashlight passing at the base of the wall.

Tink. Tink. He kneels and touches a perfectly rectangular rock formation that looks like an oversized stone vault. He places his hands on the unnatural structure and pushes upward. The thin top shifts backward from the force.

"Mr. Strauss."

Jeb jumps from the sound and turns with his revolver firmly in his hand. He grits his teeth, looking at the men who have become unwelcome guests in this search. Square Jaw leans against a tall column of rock that extends from the floor to the ceiling.

"You are not an astute, man. I thought our first encounter would have deterred you from seeking riches that weren't yours," Square Jaw says with his pistol trained on him.

"Obviously your greed is more powerful than your intellect." Square jaw continues.

Square Jaw steps away from the wall and walks toward him. The slender one emerges from behind a stalagmite glaring at Jeb. Jeb moves his index finger to the trigger and steps backward. The stone wall presses into his back.

Nowhere to go this way, he thinks, looking from Square Jaw to the seven other men in the room. He is trapped like a bird in a cage If he does try running, eight guns are going to fire away at him, and it will resemble a shooting gallery. *How am I getting out of this?*

"You see your predicament," Square Jaw jeers. "Eight against one aren't good odds."

"I'll take my chances."

"Words of a fool." Square Jaw laughs. "And I figured you for a fool when we met at Sunset Rock."

"I should have finished you there," Jeb says.

"You could finish nothing. You and your fat friend were trespassing on ancient lands."

Jeb senses his anger growing. He would probably plug him with that nine millimeter he's holding without batting an eye.

"I forgot you and your brotherhood are protecting the native treasures one rock at a time," Jeb says.

Jeb inches left. The stone rectangular slab scrapes against his calves. If he could get to the far end of the structure, he might have a chance. At least, it would give him some cover.

"How long you boy scouts been protecting this stuff? Because you play like you're amateurs. I guess the chiefs sent out the D team hoping it would work out." Jeb smiles moving another step, "I guess they can't expect too much from you."

The tall and slender man rushes forward with the barrel leveled at Jeb.

"Looks like someone wants to be the new team captain, buddy," Jeb says.

"Let's kill him now!" the tall skinny man yells.

"Have you ever fired a gun?" Jeb says. "I bet you haven't, and when you miss, that bullet is going to be bouncing off these walls like a pinball. The chance of it hitting you instead of me is quite high."

"I won't miss," Skinny says.

"That's a wager I would take."

"Enough!" Square Jaw yells.

"I want to kill this devil," Skinny replies.

Skinny and Square Jaw stare at each other, and Jeb shuffles further toward the corner. The shadows are thicker, and the slab creates a nice place to hide from the hail of bullets that will soon be erupting.

"We will kill him."

"You see." Jeb laughs. "He doesn't think you boys can shoot either. I can see the fear in his eyes. He's afraid you noobs will miss and hit him. Now that leaves us all in a quite a predicament."

"Shut up," Skinny says.

Jeb is a few feet from the corner, and the space between the rectangular slab and wall is much larger than he thought. It is five feet wide, and a small sliver of light shines from the edge of the rectangular box. He inches closer keeping his eyes on Skinny and Square Jaw.

"I want to kill him," Skinny says.

Skinny draws a long knife from a sheath attached to his belt, and he approaches Jeb with the gun pointed at him and the knife glinting in the beam of the flashlights.

Jeb's eyes dart from Skinny and his shiny blade to the small sliver of hope in the rock. There is a gap between the lid and the side panel, and it looks like it has been opened.

Jeb looks at Skinny. He twirls the knife in his hand ready to strike. Jeb only has one shot at this, and then the whole room will break loose in a flurry of chaos. Jeb licks his lips and puts pressure on the trigger with his index finger. Fire erupts from the tip of his thirty-eight. With wide eyes, Skinny looks down at the patch of red forming on his shirt. He drops the knife and staggers forward slowly.

Jeb drops to the ground as Square Jaw and the others unleash their fury. Jeb hears the bullets bouncing off the stony surfaces, and he crawls to the sliver of light and pulls on the side with all his might. The stone shifts, opening the small gap wider.

Jeb looks frantically around the smoke-filled cavern. Skinny lays a few feet away with a pool of blood collecting under his prone body.

"Where is he?" Square Jaw yells somewhere in the smoke. "I can't see him."

"He can't have gotten far. This room isn't that big."

Through the haze, one of the men steps through. Jeb fires his revolver quickly striking the man in the chest, sending him crumpling to the floor. Always aim for center mass was what he was taught, and he had been two for two so far.

"He's there!" Square Jaw yells.

A wave of bullets strikes the wall behind him, showering Jeb with bits of rock and dust. He stifles a cough and twists around, wrenching on the rock doorway. The rock slides open, and a small passage large enough for him to fit through waits for him. A bullet strikes the rectangular platform inches from his face.

Jeb drops to his belly and squirms through the narrow opening toward a faint glowing yellow light. The guns still fire, and the bullets make pinging sounds against the solid rock.

"AGHHH," someone yells from the cavern. He bets that one of the men was struck by a ricocheting bullet. Three down and five left to go.

The tunnel goes in a horizontal direction under the rectangular box at the base of the wall with all of the writing. Jeb's heart pounds. If they find this tunnel, he is as good as dead if they fire into it. Jeb pushes against the wall with his feet and claws the ground with his hands inching deeper and deeper into the mountain.

The tunnel veers to the right, and the light grows brighter.

"Hey!" Square Jaw yells.

Jeb grits his teeth pulling and pushing fiercely against the stone. His fingers are raw and bleeding, but the pain doesn't register. He has to get out of this tight passage. A gun fires behind him, and he hears the bullet bouncing off the rocks like a drumstick on a xylophone.

The passage opens into another antechamber. Jeb rolls into the gold-light-filled room. He lays on his back taking deep breaths. He looks at the ceiling, and a hole the size of a beachball allows the yellow light from the rising sun to filter into the room. He has lost track of time since they began early this morning.

CHAPTER 17

REUNION

Jeb climbs to his feet and looks at the wall where the beam of light strikes the limestone surface. More writing is scrawled across the smooth stone with a few drawings bordering the words.

This will have to wait, he thinks, turning his attention to the passage entrance. Jeb reloads his revolver and stands on the side of the tunnel. If anyone pokes their head through there, he is going to end them quickly.

"What are you doing?" Madelyn whispers.

Jeb turns, pointing the revolver at her chest. She holds her hands up and backs away slowly her eyes wide with fear.

"What is that for?" she asks.

Jeb grits his teeth, shaking his head. He presses his index finger to his lips, and Madelyn nods slowly.

He turns looking down at the tunnel entrance.

"What are we looking for?" she whispers into his ear.

Jeb feels her hot breath against his neck, and her warm body against his. He runs his hand through his sweat-soaked hair. "Some unwanted guests," Jeb whispers.

Jeb glances at her, and her eyes are wide with fear.

"Oh my," she says. "They tried to kill you. Twice."

"Three times. They nearly got me in there."

"You think they will come through there?"

"I don't know."

The thought finally hits him. "How did you get down here?" he asks with his eyes trained on the opening. "Did you come through this passage?"

"No. There is a tunnel over there that leads to the cave where we came in."

"Was that you making the tapping noises?"

"Yeah. I was trying to get . . ."

Jeb strains his ears listening, but all he can hear is the steady beating of his heart and Madelyn's soft breaths in his ear. He searches for a rock that he can lodge against the tunnel, but the small chamber doesn't have any loose rocks.

"We will need to keep an eye on both openings," Jeb whispers.

"Are we giving up on the treasure?"

"I think five guys with guns trumps a handful of gold."

"I think it is more than a handful."

Jeb turns, and her fearful wide eyes have changed. Her eyes dance like a child's when they have done something extraordinary and want their parents' approval. A thin smile curls at the edge of her mouth.

"Did you find something?" Jeb asks.

Madelyn shrugs her shoulders. "I think so," she replies. "I've never done this before, so it is exhilarating. Like a real Indiana Jones movie."

"What is it?"

"A large stone chest with the V on it. That's what I was tapping on."

His heart jumps against his ribs. The excitement of finding John Ross's treasure flows over him like a colossal wave, taking the thoughts about Square Jaw and the others away from his mind. "Show me," he says.

Madelyn leads him to the other side of the room where a tall flat wall is adorned with sentence form characters written across it. At the base of the wall sits the stone chest. Jeb leans over the rock crate and traces the V with his finger.

The box is the size of a small shipping crate. Jeb estimates it is six feet long and three feet wide. He imagines how much gold and silver lie under the thick stone lid.

"Should we open it?" Madelyn whispers.

Jeb glances from the box to Madelyn, staring wide-eyed at the stone container. Tapping the lid of the box, he tries to think about what should be done. The five protectors or whatever they call themselves are somewhere in these caverns with them, and they know the layout if what they say is true.

"I wish there was another way out of this place."

The circular beam of sunlight from the hole in the roof shines on the stone container. Jeb looks up at the opening high up in the cavern. That might be an option, but the ropes are still tied to the cliff face outside.

"We're going back the way you came," Jeb says.

"But you said."

"I know, but there isn't another way out."

"We should do this quickly."

Jeb grabs the thick lid with his hands and pushes. A piercing scraping sound fills the room, and the stone lid falls onto the rocky floor with a *thud*.

"Oh my," Madelyn says beside him.

The sunlight from the roof shines like a spotlight on the shiny contents of the box. Jeb runs his fingers through his hair and licks his lips repeatedly.

"It is so beautiful," Madelyn says, reaching her hand into the crate. The gold and silver coins and bars reflect the radiant sunlight. "That is a lot of gold and silver."

"Yep," Jeb replies with his eyes fixed on the treasure box.

The coins jingle as Madelyn moves her hand through the pieces of gold and silver. Jeb turns and looks at the passage leading back toward the cave entrance. They don't have much time to load up the loot and make a dash for the exit. There is no way to get all of it, but he will carry as much as his pack will hold.

He quickly removes his pack and kneels beside the box. "Fill it up." They alternate grabbing handfuls of coins and stowing them in the canvas bag. After six loads, Jeb lifts the bag. The weight has increased significantly.

"I think that is all we will be able to carry and still be able to go fast," Jeb says, closing the top and putting on the backpack. The weight of the bag causes the straps to cut into his shoulders.

"You got it?" Madelyn asks.

"He nods slowly. Time to get out of here."

"What about the rest?"

"We'll leave some for the next adventurer," Jeb says.

He adjusts the straps and moves toward through the long passageway at the far corner of the room. "How long did it take you to get down here?" Jeb asks.

"I don't know. Thirty minutes. I would guess."

Jeb looks into the dark tunnel, listening intently. He turns to Madelyn and holds his finger to his lips. She nods, and he walks into the gloomy passageway. The shadows grow larger and more enveloping with each step along the rocky path. It is like walking through a tube made of solid limestone, and the sound of their feet striking the wet rock is amplified in the passage.

"There are five of them waiting somewhere up ahead," Jeb whispers. Madelyn touches his arm and looks at him wide-eyed. He can see a bit of fear in her eyes, and he instinctively places his hand on hers. "We will make it." He smiles. "Trust me."

She nods her head slowly pulling out her forty-five. He had forgotten about her carrying a larger weapon than his, and he feels that they have a fighting chance. Five on two is doable.

They walk in the diminishing light up the sloping tunnel. Jeb can barely see Madelyn, but he can hear her fast short breaths and smell lavender mixed with the mustiness of the cave. The pack grows heavier with each step, and his shoulders sag under the hefty weight of the silver and gold.

Ahead, faint scraping sounds reaches his ears. He gropes in the darkness and wraps his fingers around her arm. Jeb holds her firmly, and they both stop.

"They are up ahead," he whispers in her ear. The sound of their steps grow louder like sandpaper against coarse wood. His heart pounds in his chest. They are coming, and they have nowhere to go.

They have a forty-five and a fully loaded thirty-eight and the element of surprise. He quietly backs toward the cave wall, pulling her beside him.

"Try not to make a sound," he whispers in her ear. "When they pass, we shoot and run." He hopes that they don't walk into them in the darkness or turn on a flashlight. That will destroy the plan before it starts.

The ragged slow breaths drift through the darkness, and their boots slap against the wet cave floor. He holds his breath, not wanting to give away his position as the air leaves his nostrils. Jeb squeezes Madelyn's arm and feels the tense muscles stretched tight beneath her skin.

The first member of Square Jaw's band passes them in the dark passage. The second one is a few paces behind, and his footfalls are much louder than the first. How much longer? Jeb's chest burns and his mind swims from lack of oxygen.

Jeb grits his teeth and closes his eyes. The seconds tick by slowly like time has ceased. Finally, the fifth man walks by them. His boots scrape against the exposed rock. The sound stops abruptly, and Jeb hears his breath drawing nearer.

"HEY!" the firth man yells in the darkness.

"JEB!" Madelyn screams as something metallic clatters to the rocky floor.

Her arm twists in his hands. "I got him. Them," the voice says. Jeb's finger moves to the trigger, but he can't see where he is aiming. He doesn't want to hit Madelyn. He pulls her arm forcefully, but he can't budge her. He only has a few seconds before the others are on them.

Jeb shoves the gun into his belt and takes the flashlight out of the side pocket of his pack. He presses the button on the light, bathing the tunnel in a bright golden light. The flashlight clatters to the floor, bouncing and spinning on the stone. Jeb shields his eyes from the vibrant, burning light. He squints through the blurriness pulling the thirty-eight from his belt. He fires quickly at the short muscular man wrenching Madelyn's arm.

"AGH!" he yells falling backward.

He fires again toward the others rushing toward them. The explosion from the muzzle sounds like a cannon, and Jeb's ears ring. He pulls Madelyn toward him.

"Let's go," he yells. She wrenches her arm from his grasp and scrambles to the floor. "Come on!" Jeb yells, firing another shot. The bullet strikes another attacker, sending him screaming to the floor.

Fire erupts down the tunnel. Bullets bounce off the walls above their heads, showering them in bits of rock. Madelyn fires her forty-five, dropping the man on the right side of the tunnel. She scrambles to her feet and runs with her head down toward him.

"Hurry!" Jeb screams.

Madelyn races by, and he hurries up the passage after her. Bullets whiz by them, striking the walls and ceiling.

"YOU WON'T MAKE IT OUT OF HERE ALIVE, STRAUSS," Square Jaw yells behind him.

The air thickens with the mixture of smoke from the barrels and the dust from the pulverized rock. Jeb coughs loudly, stumbling up the steadily inclining passageway. The weight of the pack presses on his shoulders, sending shots of pain into his upper and lower back. He glances backward, and the glow of the flashlight far down in the tunnel illuminates Square Jaw and his accomplice.

Jeb raises his thirty-eight and fires. The two men scurry toward the edges of the cave, hugging the smooth rock. He presses his finger against the trigger, but a metal clicking comes from the gun. Empty. Jeb turns and runs. Square Jaw and the other man hurry after him.

The tunnel erupts in a hail of fire, and Jeb ducks low, stumbling up the stone passageway. He sees the bright light from the sun filtering into the cave entrance ahead. He might just make it. As soon as the thought enters his mind, a powerful punch presses into his back slamming him forward.

"AGH!" Jeb screams, falling forward onto his knees.

Jeb blinks, looking ahead at the entrance ten yards ahead of him. He checks his arm, and blood soaks through his shirt and drips onto the cave floor. His shoulder burns, and his head throbs.

"We told you," Square Jaw says. "You will not make it out of this cave alive."

Jeb tries to stand, but a blow to his head knocks him forward onto the cold stone. The air is hazy, and his head swims. The pain in his shoulder throbs with the beat of his heart. He rolls onto his back, and Square Jaw glares at him. The barrel of the pistol is inches from his face.

"You will be buried here just like Martyn Gale," Square Jaw says coldly.

Jeb's head snaps backward, and blood flows like a torrent over his right eye. Square Jaw smiles looking at his bloody fist. Jeb sees the sinister smile through his unimpaired left eye. "We will get your girlfriend next." He laughs.

The blood flows onto the ground from his battered face. With another jolt, Jeb falls to the ground striking his head against the limestone floor. His head feels like it is ready to split open. He pushes off the ground and wipes the blood from his face. "You got me. That's all you need."

"No can know about this sanctuary. You and the girl will die, and the secret will die with you both."

Square Jaw grabs his collar and pulls Jeb upward. Jeb smells the stench of sweat and blood all around him. Their faces are inches apart, and he can see the veins on the Square Jaw's face pulse.

"The gold is ours and no thief will ever claim it," Square Jaw sneers.

Jeb blinks his eyes slowly. "We left you some."

His head jerks backward, and the room spins in slow motion. He tastes the iron from the blood in his mouth. He tries to focus his eyes on anything, but he cannot. Square Jaw's face swims in and out of focus.

"Now it is time for you to die."

Jeb waits for the final blow or the final shot that will end his treasure-hunting career and his life. It has been a good run. Four treasures in three years. An ear-splitting bang fills the rocky corridor. Jeb falls to the floor, blinking his eyes slowly. His eardrums throb from the reverberations of the explosion in the enclosed space.

Square Jaw looks at his chest, and a small red stain emerges from his shirt and quickly grows. He falls to his knees, and his eyes are blank. Another explosion comes from behind Jeb, and immediately the last remaining adversary drops to the ground.

Jeb pushes himself off the rocky ground. His head feels like it is filled with lead weights, and he braces his arm against the limestone floor.

"JEB!" Madelyn screams, falling beside him. She pulls his head upward looking into his eyes.

"You're always leaving," Jeb says.

"I always come back." She smiles.

"I guess you do. Help me up."

Madelyn wraps her arms around his chest, and he pulls himself upward. Jolts of pain shoot through his ribs and radiate into his back and shoulder. The weight of the gold-laden pack increases the amount of pain he feels. He grits his teeth. Looking at the blood soak cloth near his shoulder, Jeb shakes his head.

"This is a first."

"What is that?"

"First time I've been shot," he says. "I don't like it."

They lean against the wall and Madelyn examines his shoulder. "You were lucky," she says. "The bullet grazed you, is all."

Jeb nods, and the pain seems to increase with his back and shoulders pressed against the cold rock.

"Let's get out of here," he says.

"What about them?"

Jeb looks down at the lifeless members of the brotherhood laying on the cave floor. They have protected this secret for almost two hundred years. They dedicated their lives to the preservation of John Ross's treasure. The pack sags heavily on his shoulders as he looks at the dark hallow eyes of Square Jaw.

"They can protect the rest of the gold," Jeb says.

He walks toward the sunlit opening resting his arm on her shoulder. Each step is a challenge, but he is relieved to leave the cave. Jeb never dreamed he would face this much adversity in locating a local Tennessee legend, but the more treasures that he seeks to find the more he realizes danger is always there.

CHAPTER 18

REFLECTIONS

The late August heat makes the valley feel like an oven. The air is hot and stale, leaving the river smooth like glass. The houseboat is motionless on the water, and Jeb sits looking at the cloudless pale blue sky. He touches his face, and the skin near his eye and nose is still tender. He looks like a prize fighter who has just finished a bout with a heavy weight champion. The skin is purple and swollen.

He takes a deep breath, and the pain in his ribs and shoulder still remains. "Jeb." He doesn't try to turn his head.

"Hey, Carl."

"Boy you look terrible."

Carl sits across the table from him, staring at his battered face. "You should see the other guy," Jeb replies.

"This isn't any way to live your life."

The words are sincere, and he knows that Carl is simply looking out for him. Jeb appreciates his neighbor and his candid assessment of the life he lives. "I'm not a suit, Carl. No matter what. I never will be that." Jeb looks out at the water drifting by the pillars of the bridge that span the Tennessee River.

"A suit doesn't look like this," Carl says, pointing at the bruises on his face.

Jeb looks from the greenish blue water to Carl. His eyes are sorrowful, and Jeb can see the worry in the wrinkles of the old man's face.

"A suit never finds something like this." Jeb smiles, tossing a gold coin on the table. Carl's eyes follow the coin until it stops in front of him. The coin is embossed with the face of a bear and small lettering circle the large head. "It is beautiful. Things like that could never be found working in some office," Jeb says.

Carl touches the coin with his fingers and looks at him. A smile spreads across his face. "No. You could not." He removes the coin from the table and holds it close to his eye. "This is extraordinary. The definition and the quality of the coin is . . ."

"Unmatched."

"Yes," Carl replies.

"The Cherokee took pride in their craft."

"How many of these did you find?"

"There was an entire stone crate filled with silver and gold coins exactly like that one."

"Wow."

Carl's eyes are bright as he turns the coin over and over in his fingers. Jeb smiles, watching his friend examine the relic. "You got a crate filled with these things. How much do you think they're worth?"

"The curator at the John Ross Museum said they were priceless."

Carl eyes him suspiciously. "You showed them one?"

Jeb smiles. "I have a friend who thought the rightful owners should have the treasure returned to them."

"You gave it to them?"

Jeb nods his head and looks at the lazy current of the river. His mind drifts from the water to his adventure with Madelyn. The trip back from the mountain cave was long, and he had labored under the weight of all the gold up the ropes and along the trail to the car. Madelyn asked him numerous questions about his motivation and his desires. What he wanted out of life and why he searched for treasure.

With the answers, Madelyn looked at him and said, "You are not a greedy man, Jeb Strauss. You search for truth, and you search for things that people have lost. I don't think you hunt for treasure to make yourself rich or for fame. I think you do this to honor the people who either lost or hid their riches. That is why I admire you. That is why I like spending time with you. You aren't like everyone else in this world. Looking for the next payday or the next title. You are different, and that is refreshing."

Carl slides the coin across the table. Jeb glances at it. "Keep it," he says, smiling. "They let me keep a few more."

Carl takes the coin from the table and stows it in his pocket. "You are crazy. You know that."

"Maybe," Jeb replies.

Carl stands and stares at the water. "You are an oddity, Jeb."

Jeb has been called many things, but an oddity is a first. He slowly stands and limps toward the door. "Sorry to say goodbye so soon, Carl, but I have a pressing engagement."

"With this friend of yours?"

"The very same."

"She sounds like she has got a good head on her shoulders."

Jeb smiles as he opens the door. "She does have that."

Jeb closes the door and limps across the room. Being lighter a few million dollars didn't bother him, and he actually felt relieved to give the museum the treasure and all the artifacts that he had found. Treasure hunting isn't always about gold and silver. Sometimes it's about uncovering the truth for future generations to enjoy.

www.ingramcontent.com/pod-product-compliance
Lightning Source LLC
LaVergne TN
LVHW090528110826
845146LV00003B/1020

* 9 7 9 8 2 3 4 0 4 0 7 2 5 *